The
ILLUSTRATED
Book of
FAIRY TALES

Beauty's father is caught stealing a rose
by the furious, roaring Beast

The
ILLUSTRATED
Book of
FAIRY TALES

Spellbinding stories from around the world

Retold by
NEIL PHILIP

Illustrated by
NILESH MISTRY

DK PUBLISHING, INC.

A DK PUBLISHING BOOK

Senior Art Editor
Jacquie Gulliver

Senior Editor
Alastair Dougall

Designer
Robin Hunter

DTP Designer
Nicola Studdart

Picture Research
Sharon Southren
Christine Rista
Kate Duncan

Research
Robert Graham
Natasha Billing

Production
Josie Alabaster
Louise Barratt

Managing Art Editor
Peter Bailey

Managing Editor
Anna Kruger

US Editor
Camela Decaire

for Cortina and Rosie

First American Edition, 1997

2 4 6 8 10 9 7 5 3 1

Published in the United States by DK Publishing, Inc., 95 Madison Avenue, New York, New York 10016

Visit us on the World Wide Web at http://www.dk.com

Copyright © 1997

Dorling Kindersley Limited, London
Text copyright © 1997 Neil Philip

ISBN 0-7894-2794-X

A catalog record is available from the Library of Congress.

Color reproduction by Colourscan, Singapore
Printed and bound in Spain by Artes Graficas Toledo, S.A.
D.L. TO: 999-1997

Contents

A princess hurls a frog across her room – and is pleasantly surprised – in "The Frog Prince"

Love becomes a game of hide and seek in "The Heart's Door"

The witch cuts off Rapunzel's golden hair in "Rapunzel"

There is something very strange about grandma in "Little Red Riding Hood"

A cook hears cries coming from a dead whale, cuts it open, and out crawls a girl in "The Girl Who Combed Pearls"

A business deal has an unusual witness in "The Fly"

Heroes & Heroines

A little man helps a poor girl spin straw into gold for the king in "Rumpelstiltskin"

True Love Conquers All

A girl escapes from a fiendish witch who relentlessly pursues her in "Baba Yaga"

A king finds that a fisherman and a cottager's daughter can make a fool of him in "The Poor Girl Who Became Queen"

Introduction

THE CLASSIC fairy tales – "Cinderella," "Snow White," "Little Red Riding Hood" – are among the first stories we encounter as children. These stories, with their magic and wonder, cast an unforgettable spell – a spell that can last a lifetime.

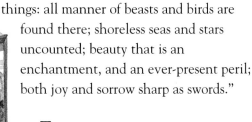

Cinderella's stepmother and stepsisters treat her like a servant

When, at the end of a fairy tale, we are told that the characters "lived happily ever after," we readily believe it. The optimism of fairy tales, in which the good overcome the wicked and the humble outwit the proud, gives hope to everyone who reads them.

However fairy tales are much more than just wish-fulfillment fantasies. Fairy-tale heroes and heroines achieve perfect happiness only after many trials and tribulations have been overcome, and fairy tales find room for grief as well as joy. As *Lord of the Rings* author J. R. R. Tolkien wrote: "The realm of fairy-story is … filled with many things: all manner of beasts and birds are found there; shoreless seas and stars uncounted; beauty that is an enchantment, and an ever-present peril; both joy and sorrow sharp as swords."

THE COLLECTION

The fairy tales chosen for this book are *all* traditional stories (tales that have been created by writers, such as Hans Christian Andersen, are not included). The selection combines classic tales made famous by Europeans such as Charles Perrault and the Brothers Grimm alongside others from many different cultures.

The Frog Prince agrees to fetch the princess's ball

Before our tales were first collected in books, they, and thousands of others, had been told around the world's firesides and hearths for centuries. In bygone times, many people could not read, so storytelling was a vital part of their entertainment and also education. For example, telling a fairy tale such as "Little Red Riding Hood" was a thoroughly memorable way for a parent to warn children not to talk to strangers. When the children grew up, they might tell the same story to their own children. And so tales were handed down from generation to generation.

The wolf licks its lips when it sees Little Red Riding Hood

The fairy tales in this book have been grouped together to show how similar themes recur all over the world. Care has also been taken to place each one in a suitable visual setting. Details of landscape, costume, and design have been

Soliday shoots the monstrous Man-Crow

considered to make the illustration that accompanies each tale magical and authentic.

TALES FOR THE TELLING

Fairy tales are meant to be shared. An old Korean tale tells of a boy who loved to be told stories, but never told them to others. The boy hoarded stories like a miser hoards coins. Every time he heard a new one, he put its spirit into an old purse, which was soon full to bursting.

At last the boy was old enough to marry. On the morning of his wedding, his servant heard whispers coming from the old purse. The imprisoned story spirits were muttering angrily among themselves. "We're suffocating in here. But what does he care? Today is our chance to get our own back!"

One spirit suggested that a bush of poisonous strawberries would tempt the boy on the way to his wedding. Another spirit hoped that he might burn himself on a red-hot poker. Finally, a third spirit said that, if all else failed, a snake in the bridal chamber would surely bite him to death!

The servant, hearing all this, was able to prevent each of these disasters. After he had cut off the snake's head, he told his master that he had heard the imprisoned story spirits plotting against him.

"It's not natural, keeping them confined like that," he said. "You must set them free."

The young man realized his mistake,

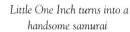

Little One Inch turns into a handsome samurai

untied the old purse, and let the story spirits out. And from that day on, he told his stories to anyone who would listen.

Writing fairy stories down in a book is a bit like tying them up in an old purse. There is a danger they might suffocate. Open up the book, and set the story spirits free!

The Story of Fairy Tales

FOR AS LONG AS HISTORY, people have told each other fairy tales. A papyrus dating from around 1700 BC reveals that the pharaoh Cheops, builder of Egypt's Great Pyramid, was fond of fairy tales, and the surviving fairy tales of ancient Egypt show many striking similarities to modern stories. One, "Anpu and Bata," has much in common with the Congolese story "The Twin Brothers" in this book; the plot of "The Twin Brothers" is, in turn, similar to the German tale "The Gold Children," retold by the Brothers Grimm, and to stories from Russia, Greece, Italy, Ireland, Chile, and elsewhere.

Fairy tales are found all over the world – among the English and the Inuit, the Americans and the Ainu. Many of them are clearly very old, because the same plots and plot details recur in different cultures and on different continents. But if fairy tales are old, they are also always being made new. Whenever someone says – or, nowadays, writes – "Once upon a time...," a fairy tale comes to life, as fresh as the first time it was ever told.

The timeless, dreamlike imagery of fairy tale, portrayed by John Anster in The Stuff That Dreams Are Made Of

Magical transformations are a key fairy-tale ingredient. This study of a man turning into a frog is by Jean Grandville

"The Girl Who Pretended To Be a Boy," the heroine even changes from female to male – and marries the princess.

Added to this topsy-turvy world is one of fairy tale's most vital, timeless ingredients: magic – capable of turning a pumpkin into a coach, sending a princess to sleep for a hundred years, or, in the hands of the wicked, turning a prince into a beast. Magic in fairy tales mirrors the human imagination, where just to *think* something is to make it real. In "The Frog Prince," a slimy frog suddenly becomes a handsome prince; in "The Lame Fox," a fox turns herself, in turn, into a golden girl, a golden horse, and a golden apple tree. In

In some ways, fairy tales resemble dreams, flowing from image to image or scene to scene with the same magical speed and transporting the reader in a flash to places where literally anything can happen.

Once we step beyond the threshold of "Once upon a time..." – we enter a world where, as in dreams, reality appears topsy-turvy. Suddenly, animals can not only talk, but, like the cat in "Puss in Boots," are far cleverer than human beings. The poorest, simplest, laziest, most good-for-nothing rascal, such as the Ash Lad of "An Eating Match With a Troll" or Jack of "Jack & the Beanstalk," becomes a daring, irresistible hero, capable of the most wonderful feats. At the end of a Romanian story,

In a fairy tale, the landscape can take on a life of its own. This unusual painting is by an anonymous 16th-century Dutch artist

The hero of "The Wonderful Brocade" travels to fairyland on a magic steed

"Baba Yaga," a girl fleeing from a witch drops a towel – it becomes a broad river. When that does not stop the witch she flings a comb behind her – it becomes a forest so dense the witch cannot chew her way through it, and the girl escapes to her father's hut.

Talking animals are not at all unusual in fairy tales. This illustration from "Puss in Boots" is by Warwick Goble

It is because fairy tales speak so clearly to our imaginations as well as to our hearts that they have remained so popular. The influence of classic stories such as "Cinderella," "The Sleeping Beauty," "Bluebeard," and "The Frog Prince" echoes and reechoes through modern films, novels, poems – even advertising.

❦ FAIRY-TALE JUSTICE

The real world is rarely fair, but in fairy tales the good are nearly always well rewarded and the wicked severely punished. Even death itself cannot stand in the way of a just and happy ending. Although the wicked queen in "Snow White" appears to have killed the heroine with a poisoned apple, when the piece of apple luckily falls out of Snow White's mouth, she comes alive again. She marries the prince and the wicked queen meets a fittingly gruesome fate.

Brave St. George rescues a princess from an evil dragon. This classic image of fairy-tale heroism is attributed to the 14th-century artist Altichieri

This sense that at the root of life there is such a thing as natural justice is a powerful part of fairy tales' appeal. But they are enjoyed, too, for their sheer excitement. Their monsters and villains make us shiver; and we suffer with their heroes

A fairy godmother such as Mother Goose (painted by Arthur Rackham) embodies goodness

Evil may be represented by a hideous witch mixing up magic potions to harm the innocent, as depicted by Hans Thoma

Fairy-tale heroes can be princes or paupers – such as the Norwegian Ash Lad, here shown teasing a troll in an illustration by Theodor Kittlesen

On October 14, 1892, the Irish poet W. B. Yeats visited a place that was widely believed to be a fairy haunt and invoked the fairies. The very next day he wrote, "Once there was a great sound as of little people cheering & stamping with their feet in the heart of the rock. The queen of the troop came then – I could see her – & held a long conversation with us & finally wrote in the sand 'be careful & do not seek to know too much about us.' "

Scary creatures, like this jinn illustrated by René Bull, are a major part of fairy tales' appeal

Such a warning may serve for all those who try to explain away or pour scorn on fairies or fairy tales. After all the scholarly theories of fairy tales' hidden meanings, the tales are still there – pure, untouched, and full of mystery. And perhaps the fairies are, too.

and heroines and rejoice when everything comes right. Most enticing of all, fairy tales are full of wonders – even if fairies do not always appear!

THE "GOOD PEOPLE"

Fairies are part of many countries' folklore, and belief in them was once widespread, particularly in rural areas. It was said that the fairies were spirits, or fallen angels, or the descendants of the children that Eve hid in the shadows from God, or the remnants of an earlier race of beings. They were thought to have little sympathy for humankind and to exact terrible revenge on anyone who offended them. Country folk called them "the good people" as a mark of respect.

The fairies are always with us – a typical image of fairyland from Shakespeare's A Midsummer Night's Dream, painted by William Blake

The Storytellers

FAIRY TALES ARE living things. They have been handed down through generations for centuries. At first they were passed on by word of mouth at a time when many people could not read or write and lived in isolated farms and villages. Later, when schools opened and more families moved to towns, the old storytelling ways were in danger of coming to an end. Then, it was the turn of the collectors to preserve the stories by listening to storytellers and writing down their words. Although time may have changed some of the tales in the telling, they continue to delight, entertain, and even frighten young listeners the world over. Today, the magic of fairy tales is rekindled when parents read to their children, or when the family is captivated by a film such as Walt Disney's *Snow White and the Seven Dwarfs*. In much the same way, generations ago, children listened open-mouthed as grandparents spun tales by the warmth of the fire, while shadows flickered on the walls.

A handsome frontispiece to an early 20th-century French edition of Charles Perrault's tales

Tale-spinning the traditional way: a family gathers around the fire to listen to grandma's story in A Winter Night's Tale *by Daniel Maclise*

CHARLES PERRAULT

The modern writing down of tales dates from 1697 when *Stories, or Tales of Past Times*, by Frenchman Charles Perrault (1628–1703), was published. A man of letters and civil servant – he helped oversee the building of Louis XIV's palace at Versailles and the Louvre – he concealed his authorship, and the book was attributed to his teenage son, Pierre. Its eight traditional fairy tales, which included "Cinderella," "Sleeping Beauty," "Little Red Riding Hood," "Puss in Boots," and "Bluebeard," started a craze for fanciful, made-up stories.

Left: The Brothers Grimm: Wilhelm (left) and Jacob. The brothers were orphans who were well educated thanks to a generous aunt

Right: the cover of this late-19th-century German collection of Grimms' fairy tales features Snow White and the seven dwarfs

THE BROTHERS GRIMM

In the early 19th century, German brothers Wilhelm (1786–1859) and Jacob (1785–1863) Grimm followed Perrault's lead and began to collect traditional fairy tales from their family and friends. Wilhelm's future wife, Dortchen Wild, contributed more than a dozen stories, including "Rumpelstiltskin," and family friends Jeannette and Amalie Hassenpflug gave them "Snow White." The brothers also discovered a remarkable storyteller in her fifties named Dorothea Viehmann, who told them many stories, including "The Twelve Brothers" (similar to "The Unknown Sister" in this book). Grimms' fairy tales soon found their way into the homes and hearts of children all over Europe.

The Grimms' success encouraged others to try to preserve for posterity the riches of world folklore. Intrepid collectors tracked down gifted storytellers in every continent in order to record their tales in their exact words.

HANS CHRISTIAN ANDERSEN

The Grimms inspired writers to create new tales in traditional fairy-tale form. The most famous of these writers is Hans Christian Andersen (1805–75). The son of a poor shoemaker, he was brought up in a hospital in Odense, Denmark, where he often listened, enthralled, to the old women's stories as they worked in the spinning room. Andersen's tales, which include "The Ugly Duckling" and "The Snow Queen," are made-up, literary works, and so are not included in this traditional story collection.

Hans Christian Andersen, painted by Albert Küchler

Today, although fewer people tell stories by word of mouth, a gifted storyteller can still

Since the 1930s, Walt Disney's animated films have introduced children to many traditional fairy tales, such as Sleeping Beauty

hold an audience spellbound, and we can also listen to stories on radio or tape, read them ourselves, or watch them on film and video. The magical spell cast by fairy tales shows no sign of losing its power.

Under a Spell

Many characters in fairy tales, such as Beast in "Beauty and the Beast," are under a spell. They have been transformed by magic, often into the shape of an animal. It is the task of the hero or heroine to recognize the essential person behind the spell; in the end Beauty's courage and willingness to love Beast for his inner goodness breaks the spell. Most fairy tales about people under a spell end with the cruel enchantment being broken, but not all, as the story "Why the Sea Moans" shows. Usually a spell must work itself out, for good or ill, like the workings of fate. When Urashima in "Urashima & the Turtle" falls under a spell of eternal youth, his happiness is fated to end when he opens the fairy casket and ages hundreds of years in seconds.

In the beautiful Inuit story "A Whale's Soul & Its Burning Heart," the spell that is broken by the raven's meddling is nothing less than life itself, the most precious and most fragile magic spell of all.

The fairy princess gives Urashima a box and warns him not to open it if he wishes to return to her

The Sleeping Beauty

TIMELESS TALE
The tale of "The Sleeping Beauty" dates back at least to the 14th century. However the best-known version was set down by Frenchman Charles Perrault in 1697 under the title *La Belle au Bois Dormant.* This version formed the basis for later retellings (by the Brothers Grimm and others), including this one.

FAIRY-TALE CASTLE
Built in 1462 as a fortress and later ornamented with turrets, towers, and windows, the Chateau of Ussé inspired Perrault to write "The Sleeping Beauty." It overlooks the Indre River in western France.

ONCE UPON A TIME a king and queen longed for a child. Year after year they waited and at last they had a daughter. Overcome with joy, the royal parents asked seven fairies to be godmothers to the little princess. They knew that if the fairies each gave the child a gift, as was the custom, she would grow to be the most perfect princess in the whole world.

The youngest fairy

The royal couple and the fairies cower in fear, but the youngest fairy hides behind a curtain

At the christening feast each fairy godmother was given a plate, knife, and fork of solid gold. But just as the guests sat down, an eighth fairy, ugly and shriveled with age, entered the hall. No one had seen her for fifty years and so she had not been invited. The king could not give her a gold plate, a gold knife, and a gold fork because only seven sets had been made, so the old fairy grumbled and muttered, believing herself insulted. To undo any evil the old fairy might be planning, the youngest fairy decided to save her gift until last, and hid.

The feast over, the fairies presented their gifts to the princess. The first gave her the gift of beauty; the next of wisdom. The other fairies declared that she would be exquisitely graceful, a superb dancer, a wonderful singer, and a skilled musician. Then the old fairy croaked spitefully: "The princess will prick her finger on a spindle and die!"

At this the youngest fairy stepped forward and said: "The princess will not die! When she pricks her finger, she will fall into a deep sleep. She shall slumber a hundred years, when a prince shall come to wake her." This was not enough for the king. He ordered that every spindle should be burned, and the princess grew up safe from harm.

In a lonely tower room an old lady sits spinning thread

distaff

spindle

The king orders that every spindle be burned

The royal family leaves to spend the summer at a castle in the country

The spiteful old fairy puts a curse on the baby princess

The princess climbs a winding staircase

One summer the king and queen took her to a castle in the country. At the top of a tower she found a little room. There an old lady sat, spinning thread, using a spinning wheel and spindle. She knew nothing of the king's order. Eager to try, the princess reached out her hand. But when she took hold of the spindle, she pricked her finger and fell down in a faint…

Her eyes were shut, but her cheeks were rosy and she was breathing softly. In vain they tried to wake her. Finally the king ordered the servants to take her to the finest room in the castle.

There, on a bed embroidered with gold and silver, the princess lay like a sleeping angel.

THE FATEFUL SPINDLE
The spindle with which the princess pricks her finger might have been horizontally attached to a spinning wheel, or been a handheld type, such as the one above.

BRIAR ROSE
Grimm's version of the tale is called "Little Briar-Rose." In this title, the name of the princess combines thorns – associated with suffering and also with fairy power – with a flower that symbolizes beauty, perfection, and love.

CLASSIC BALLET
Princess Aurora (Ravenna Tucker) faints after pricking her finger in a scene from the great classical ballet *The Sleeping Beauty*, first performed in Russia in 1890 with choreography by Marius Petipa. The thrilling music by Tchaikovsky also featured in the 1959 Walt Disney cartoon.

When the youngest fairy heard what had happened, she came straight to the castle. "It is well that the princess sleeps in peace," she said, "but I am worried that, when she wakes, she will find herself among strangers."

The fairy took her wand and touched every living thing in the castle, except for the king and queen – all the servants and soldiers, the horses and watchdogs, and even the princess's own pet spaniel, Mopsie, lying next to her on the bed. They all fell asleep, too.

The king and queen sadly kissed their child good-bye and left the castle, forbidding anyone to approach it. To keep the princess safe from harm, the fairy encircled the castle with a forest of brambles and thorns so thick that no one could get through, and so high that only the very tops of the castle's turrets could be seen above the bushes.

A hundred years went by. The king and queen died, and another royal family came to rule the kingdom. One day the king's son was riding out in search of adventure when he glimpsed what looked like the towers of

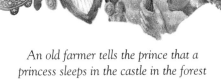

An old farmer tells the prince that a princess sleeps in the castle in the forest

a castle rising above a gloomy forest. He questioned some passersby, who agreed that the towers were indeed those of a castle. But some said it was full of ghosts, some that it was the haunt of witches, and others that a foul ogre lived there who ate children. Then an old farmer spoke up: "As a boy, I heard that a beautiful princess sleeps in that castle, waiting for the prince who will wake her!"

His heart pounding with excitement, the prince at once set out for the castle. When he reached the forest surrounding it, the thickets of brambles and thorns mysteriously parted to let him through. Then, just as mysteriously, they closed again behind him.

The thorns part, allowing the prince to pass.
All the people and animals in the courtyard are asleep

He reached the courtyard and
marveled at all the bodies of people and
animals that lay, as if dead, all around him. He went into the
guardroom and saw the guards standing in line, pikes at their
shoulders, snoring away. Then he went into each room in turn until
at last he found the chamber where the princess lay sleeping.

Amazed by her beauty, which seemed to surround her with radiance,
he fell to his knees and woke her with a kiss.

"Is it you, my prince?" she smiled. "I have waited for such a long
time." And he took her in his arms.

Meanwhile, all over the castle, men, women, and animals were
waking up. The roast was once more crackling on the spit, and even
the flies were buzzing again.

The prince and princess dined in a mirrored room to music played
on instruments that, though silent for a hundred years, still sounded
sweet and true. And the priest married them that very night, for, as
the princess said, a hundred years' wait was quite long enough!

*The prince at last finds
the room where the
princess lies sleeping*

———— ✒ ————

A STICKY END
In Perrault's version,
the story continues after
Sleeping Beauty's
marriage. The prince's
mother, an ogress with a
taste for human flesh, is
determined to eat the
princess and her two
children. When the
prince discovers the
plot, the ogress kills
herself by jumping into
a tub of snakes.

The Shape-Changer

LION TRACKS
In this tale, collected from the Akamba people of Kenya, the tracks of a lion (above) fool a buyer into thinking that his bull has been eaten.

THERE ONCE WAS A MAN named Mbokothe, who lived with his brother. Their parents had died, and left them two cows. Mbokothe said, "If I take the cows to a medicine man, he'll give me magical powers."

He drove the cows across the country to a famous medicine man, who took the cows and gave Mbokothe the power to take on the shape of any animal he chose. Mbokothe went home and told his brother, telling him to keep it a secret.

One day Mbokothe changed himself into a huge, handsome bull, and his brother drove him to market to sell him. A man paid Mbokothe's brother two cows and five goats.

On the way home Mbokothe the bull escaped from his buyer. The man chased him, but Mbokothe changed his back legs into those of a lion. When the man saw the tracks, he said sadly, "It is no use. The bull has been caught and eaten by a lion."

And Mbokothe turned back into a man and strolled home.

The next market day Mbokothe turned himself into a bull again and his brother sold him for ten goats. But Mbokothe didn't know that the man who bought him had visited the same medicine man and won magical powers of his own.

Mbokothe drives his cows to a medicine man, who gives him magical powers

When Mbokothe the bull ran off, the man turned into a lion and caught up with him. Mbokothe turned himself into a bird and flew away, but the man quickly became a powerful kite and flew after him. Mbokothe landed and changed into an antelope, but the man turned into a wolf. Every time Mbokothe changed shape, the man did, too, until Mbokothe was worn out.

"You've won," he said.

"Let's go back to my house, and I'll give you back all your goats."

Even a man of power will meet his match one day.

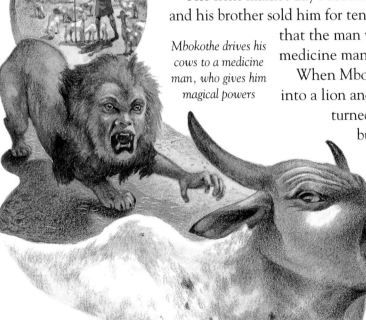

Later, Mbokothe tries to trick a man by turning into a bull, but the man – a shape-changer, too – becomes a raging lion

❧ *Little One Inch* ❧

ONCE THERE WAS a man and a woman who longed to have a child. They prayed and prayed, and eventually the gods sent them a baby boy. He was a fine, healthy baby, but he never grew, and so they called him Little One Inch.

When he was old enough, his parents sent Little One Inch out into the world, armed with a needle instead of a sword.

He sailed down the river to the capital, Kyoto, using a rice bowl as a boat and chopsticks as oars. There he was taken in by a family that lived in a big house. The family thought he was cute.

One day Little One Inch went on a journey with the

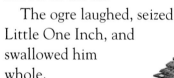

Little One Inch sails to Kyoto in a rice bowl

daughter of the house, who was fond of him. They were attacked by an ogre, who wanted to steal the girl away.

"You'll have to deal with me first!" Little One Inch shouted, waving his needle in the air.

The ogre laughed, seized Little One Inch, and swallowed him whole.

The ogre picks Little One Inch up and swallows him

Inside the ogre's stomach, Little One Inch stabbed with his needle until the ogre coughed him up. Then he jabbed the needle in the ogre's eye. The ogre howled with pain and ran away, dropping a small metal object as he did so.

"It's a magic hammer that grants wishes," cried the girl, snatching it up.

"Then hit me with it, and see if it'll make me grow," said Little One Inch.

The girl gave him a terrific smack on the head and he began to grow… Soon Little One Inch was a tall, handsome young samurai whom any girl would be pleased to marry.

PINT-SIZED HERO
Little One Inch is the Japanese equivalent of the European fairy-tale hero Tom Thumb, seen above in a 19th-century picture book being chased by Old Grumbo the giant. The Japanese ogre in this tale is an *oni*. These tusked, malevolent ogres are usually bright red or blue in color.

Little One Inch turns into a samurai

The Frog Prince

THE FAIRY-TALE FROG
In many parts of the world frogs symbolize new life, and so usually appear in stories as kind and helpful. But for Christians, the frog, like the toad, also has links with witchcraft. For a prince to be changed into a slimy frog, as in this story, is therefore to fall from being the noblest of God's creatures to one of the most despised.

WISHING WELL
It is a traditional belief that good spirits live in wells. People toss coins into wishing wells in the hope that the spirits will grant their wishes. The frog in this story lives near a well – a sign he may bring the princess good luck.

LONG AGO THERE lived a king who had a beautiful daughter. Near his castle was a forest and in the forest was a well and that was where the princess liked to play with her golden ball. One day – splash! – the ball fell into the well. The princess began to cry.

"What's wrong, princess?" croaked a voice. But there wasn't anybody there, just a frog.

"Is it you, old puddle-squelcher?" the princess sniffled. "My golden ball has fallen into the well."

"What will you give me if I fetch it?"

"Whatever you want, you dear frog," said the princess. "My clothes, my jewels – even my crown!"

The frog answered, "I don't want your clothes, your jewels, or your crown. But if you will love me and be my friend, if I can eat off your plate and sleep in your bed, then I will get your golden ball."

"I promise," said the princess. "Anything you like." The frog dived into the well. What an ugly frog, the princess thought. Only fit to sit in a pond and croak!

Soon the frog returned and in his mouth was the golden ball. Delighted, the princess snatched it up and ran home. "Wait! I can't run as fast as you!" croaked the frog.

The next day, when the princess was dining with the king, there came a knock. When she saw who it was, she slammed the door.

"Who was that, dear?" asked the king.

"A slimy frog," shuddered the princess.

"And what did the frog want?"

"Yesterday my golden ball fell down a well and this frog fetched it. In return I promised he could be my friend. I never thought he would follow me home."

The frog offers to dive in the well and fetch the princess's golden ball

"You must keep your promise," the king said. So the princess opened the door and the frog hopped in. The frog said, "Lift me up." The king told the princess to lift the frog onto the table. Then the frog said to her, "Push your plate nearer so I can share your food." The frog slurped up his share; the princess barely touched hers.

Afterward the frog said, "I'm tired. Let's go to sleep in your bed." The princess began to cry, but the king told her, "You accepted his help. You cannot turn him away."

She picked the frog up in two fingers, carried him to her room, and dropped him in a corner. But when she got into bed, the frog jumped onto her pillow and said, "I'll sleep here!"

"Let me be!" cried the princess and she threw him against the wall. To her amazement, the frog changed into a handsome prince!

"I was turned into a frog by a witch," he explained. "But your promise of love has broken the spell! Now let us sleep, and in the morning we will go to my kingdom."

The next morning a coach arrived. The coachman was the prince's old servant Henry, who had been so unhappy when his master was turned into a frog that a blacksmith had fixed three iron bands around his heart to stop it from breaking. As they drove along, the prince and princess heard a loud crack. The prince cried, "Henry, the carriage is breaking!"

"It's not the carriage, master," answered Henry. "It's an iron band from around my heart!" Twice more they heard a crack, and each time they thought the carriage was breaking, but it was only an iron band springing from around the heart of old Henry, in joy and happiness.

The princess keeps her promise and lets the frog eat from her plate

How EMBARRASSING! This story was first written down by the Brothers Grimm in the early 19th century, but its classic tale of a pretty princess highly embarrassed by a promise to a repulsive creature is probably far older, and many countries have their own versions.

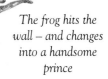
The frog hits the wall – and changes into a handsome prince

The princess hurls the frog out of her bed

Henry joyfully drives them to the prince's kingdom

The Lame Fox

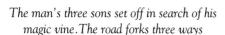

The man's right eye was always laughing and his left eye was always weeping

T HERE ONCE WAS a man who had three sons. Two were bright boys, but the youngest was a foolish lad. Now this man's right eye was always laughing, but his left eye was always weeping. The man's sons decided to ask him why this was so.

The eldest son asked, but the man threw a knife at him. The second son asked and the same thing happened. Both sons fled. Then the third son asked. The man seized his knife, but the boy did not run.

The man put down the knife and said, "My other two sons are cowards, but you are brave, so my right eye laughs. But my left eye weeps because my magic vine, which gives twenty-four buckets of wine a day, has been stolen."

The three brothers agreed to set out in search of the magic vine. The road forked three ways, and each took a path.

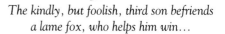

The man's three sons set off in search of his magic vine. The road forks three ways

The kindly, but foolish, third son befriends a lame fox, who helps him win…

HELPFUL FOX
The fox is celebrated as the most cunning of animals. The fox in this story, unlike foxes in most tales, is not sly or greedy, but a patient helper for the hero.

The two older boys soon met up once more. "Praise God, we've managed to shake off that ninny!" they laughed and sat down to eat the food they had brought. Along came a lame she-fox, looking very hungry. But the brothers didn't spare her a crumb; they just said, "There's a fox! Let's kill it!" The fox limped away.

When the foolish lad sat down to eat, the same fox came up to him. "These are hard times," he said. "Share my meal."

After they had eaten the fox said, "Where are you going?" The simpleton, amazed the fox could speak, told her everything.

"Follow me," said the fox.

They came to a garden. "The vine is in there," the fox said. "You must pass twelve guards. Their eyes are open, but they are asleep. You'll find a gold shovel and a wooden shovel. Dig up the vine with the wooden shovel and come back to me."

But when the lad reached the vine, he forgot what the fox had said, and took up the gold shovel. As soon as he pushed it into the ground, it woke the guards, and they took him to their master.

"But the vine is my father's," the foolish lad exclaimed.

"That's as may be," said the lord, "but I will not give it back unless you bring me the golden apple tree that bears golden fruit every day."

The lad went back to the fox and the fox said, "Follow me." She took him to another garden and said: "To reach the golden apple tree, you must pass another twelve guards. By the tree are two poles: a golden one and a wooden one. Take the wooden pole, beat the tree, and come back to me."

But the silly lad beat the tree with the golden pole and woke the guards. The lord said, "I'll give you the tree, if you bring me the golden horse with the golden wings."

The lad went back to the fox and the fox said, "Follow me." She led him through a dark forest to a farmyard

GOLDEN APPLES
Pictured here in a detail from *The Vision of the Blessed Gabriele* by Carlo Crivelli, golden apples are prized in myths and tales for bestowing eternal youth.

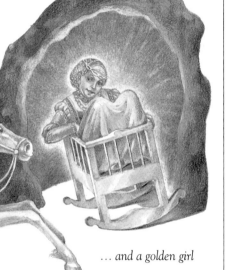

… a golden apple tree…   *… a golden horse…*   *… and a golden girl*

and said, "First you must pass twelve guards. The golden horse is in a stable and hanging near it are two bridles, one of gold and one of straw. Bridle the horse with the straw one, and ride him back to me."

But the silly lad bridled the horse with the golden bridle and woke the guards. The lord said, "I'll give you the golden horse, if you bring me the golden girl in the golden cradle."

The lad went back to the fox and the fox said, "Follow me." She took him to a cave and said, "Inside the cave, past twelve guards, is the golden girl, rocking herself in her golden cradle. Nearby is a huge specter, screaming, 'No! No!' Pay it no mind. Pick up the golden cradle, and bring it to me."

This time, the lad did as the fox said. They went back to the farmyard and the lad said, "The golden girl is so beautiful, it seems a pity to give her up." So the fox turned herself into a golden girl,

SPECIAL EYES
This story is from Bohemia, in the southern Czech Republic. A similar story is found in the fairy tales of the Brothers Grimm entitled "The Golden Bird," and also in *The Arabian Nights*. However, the detail of the one laughing eye and one crying eye is unique to central Europe.

27

The lord suddenly realizes that his golden girl has fox's eyes

TRUE TO NATURE
A human changing into an animal, and vice versa, is a common fairy-tale event, but in this story the fox does not completely change into the golden girl. The fox's true nature shines through – just like that of the main character in the La Fontaine fable "The Cat Who Changed into a Woman" (above). Although a good wife to her husband, the cat-woman just cannot help chasing mice.

except her eyes were a fox's eyes. The lad gave the fox-girl to the lord, and took away the golden horse.

That night, the lord was gazing at the golden girl when he cried out, "You have a fox's eyes!" The girl changed back into the fox, which ran to where the lad was waiting with the real golden girl and the golden horse.

The fox next changed herself into a golden horse, except she still had a fox's tail. The lad swapped her for the golden tree. Later, when the lord was admiring the horse, he said, "You are so beautiful, except for that scruffy fox's tail!" The horse changed back into the fox, which ran to where the lad was waiting.

Last the fox changed herself into a golden apple tree and the lad swapped her for his father's vine. But as the lord was admiring the tree, he suddenly said, "How strange! The apples look like fox's heads!" And the tree turned back into the fox, which ran off to join the lad, the girl, the horse, the tree, and the vine.

On the way home the lad encountered his brothers. They threw him down a well and stole his treasures. But when they took them back to their father, the vine wouldn't make wine, the apple tree wouldn't bloom, the golden horse wouldn't neigh, and the golden girl wouldn't smile. And still their father's left eye wept.

Meanwhile the lame fox rescued the lad from the well. While he lay gasping for air on the grass, she changed into a princess. She had been cursed to walk the world as a fox until she saved the life of a friend. "Now I am free," she said, "and so are you. Farewell, my friend."

The princess went her way, and the lad went home. There he told his father the whole story, and, as he did so, the vine began to make wine, the apple tree bloomed, the horse neighed, and the golden girl sang. Best of all, his father's left eye stopped weeping and began to laugh.

As the lovers embrace, the father drives out his two wicked sons

The father drove his two bad sons out, the foolish lad married the golden girl, and they lived happily ever after.

❧ Jamie Freel & the Young Lady ❧

EVERY HALLOWEEN lights were seen burning in the ruined castle and sounds of dancing and music could be heard. But no one ever went near; it was known to be a favorite haunt of the "wee folk," the fairies.

But one Halloween, Jamie Freel, a poor widow's son from Fannet, said, "I am going to the castle to seek my fortune."

His mother begged him not to go, but he was a brave lad and he strode out into the moonlit night. Wild music carried on the breeze and, as Jamie drew nearer to the old castle, he could also hear laughter and singing. The sounds were coming from the castle hall, where windows were ablaze with light. Jamie nervously peered in.

The whole fairy host, none of them taller than a child of five years, were feasting and drinking, stamping their feet and dancing, while flutes and fiddles played.

As soon as they spotted Jamie the fairies shouted, "Welcome, Jamie Freel! Welcome! We're going to Dublin tonight to steal a young lady. Will you ride with us, Jamie Freel?"

"Yes, I will," Jamie boldly replied.

FAIRY LAND
This tranquil landscape is part of the real-life setting of this fairy tale. It shows Fannad (Fannet) Head in County Donegal, Northern Ireland, with the waters of Lough Swilly on the right.

———— ❧ ————

BELIEF IN FAIRIES
At the beginning of this century it was estimated that more than ten percent of the Irish rural population genuinely believed in fairies. Fairies were often blamed for minor mishaps, such as milk turning sour. Anyone who offended the fairy folk risked serious illness, even death. It was believed to be unlucky to tell stories about fairies in the daytime.

As Jamie approaches the castle, he hears music and sees lights in the windows

*The fairies invite Jamie on
a wild nighttime ride*

So Jamie mounted a fairy horse and rode through the air with the fairy host whooping around him, over the roof of his mother's cottage, over hills, fields, and villages, over deep Lough Swilly, and past the spire of Derry Cathedral, until at last they reached Dublin. The fairies chose the finest house in Stephen's Green for their visit. The shimmering host halted by a window where a beautiful girl lay sleeping. Jamie looked on in amazement as the fairies swept into the room and stole her from her own bed.

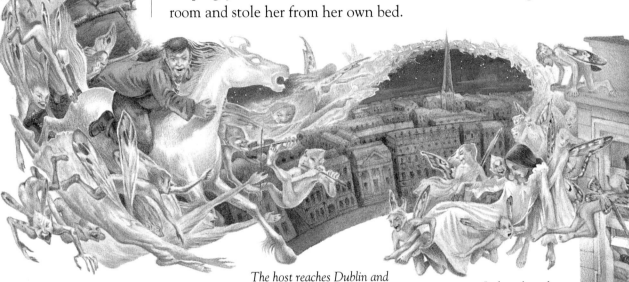

*The host reaches Dublin and
steals a beautiful girl from her bed*

*In her place they
leave a stick*

*The girl in Jamie's
arms turns into a snarling
dog, but he will not
let go*

ST. STEPHEN'S GREEN
The wealthy young lady of the story would most probably have grown up in a house like this one – a beautiful Georgian terrace in St. Stephen's Green, Dublin.

In her place, they left a stick that took on her shape, but was lifeless.

The fairies took turns carrying the girl as they galloped homeward across the starlit sky.

"Don't I get a turn?" shouted Jamie as they whirled over the village of Tamney, not far from his mother's cottage. So they gave her to him – and he jumped from his fairy mount with the girl in his arms.

The fairies pursued them, crying with rage in their high-pitched voices. Before Jamie could bundle the girl inside the cottage, they turned her into a black dog, barking and snapping; into a glowing bar of iron; into a sack of wool. But Jamie would not let go of her.

At last one fairy, a tiny woman, said, "Jamie can have her, but he shall have no good of her, for I'll make her deaf and dumb!" She sprinkled something over the girl and the fairies rushed away into the night sky. Jamie lifted the latch and entered the cottage.

"How will we look after a lady like her?" cried his mother, when he had told her of all the night's wonders.

"I'll work for you both," said Jamie, turning to the girl. But tears were rolling down her cheeks; she could neither hear nor speak.

A year passed by and Halloween came again. Jamie decided to pay another visit to the ruined castle. As he entered the hall, he overheard the tiny woman fairy say, "What a poor trick Jamie Freel played on us last year, stealing the girl from us; but at least we struck her deaf and dumb. But he does not know that just three drops from this glass in my hand would give her back her hearing and speech."

Then the fairies caught sight of Jamie and made him welcome. "Drink our health out of this glass!" cried the tiny woman. Jamie took the glass from the fairy and darted out of the hall before the fairies knew what was happening.

Jamie ran till he thought his heart would burst and at last reached home. There were just three drops left in the glass. He gave them to the girl and right away she was herself again. She couldn't thank Jamie enough, but naturally she wanted to go back home to see her mother and father. The very next day she and Jamie set off on the long walk to Dublin.

It took far longer than the fairy journey but at last they found the grand house in Stephen's Green and knocked on the door.

"The daughter of the house died a year ago!" said the servants, and refused to let them in. Jamie and the girl insisted, and finally her father came to the door. But he just said, "My daughter is dead. Go away."

"Please, leave us alone," added her mother.

Then Jamie Freel spoke up and told them all about the fairies and the piece of wood they had left in the girl's bed, and at last the mother and father began to believe that their daughter really had come back to them. Jamie's mother was fetched from Fannet in a coach and Jamie and the beautiful girl he had saved from the fairies were married in a splendid wedding.

RUINED CASTLE
Burt Castle, Inishowen, County Donegal, is typical of the many picturesque castles scattered over the Irish countryside. At night, of course, they can look distinctly forbidding, and with moonlight shining through the windows, a castle might well appear to be mysteriously lit up from within by a fairy host.

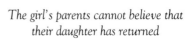

The girl's parents cannot believe that their daughter has returned

The Unknown Sister

SAVED BY SWANS
This story is of European origin, and formed the basis of Hans Christian Andersen's "The Wild Swans." In this illustration, by Anne Anderson, the heroine is being rescued by her swan-brothers.

BIRD CHANGES Story details change to suit a particular audience. Macaws are common in Suriname, so the brothers become macaws. In German versions, however, they turn into ravens.

ONCE THERE WAS a king who had twelve sons. He longed for a daughter, and he told his wife, "If we could have a daughter, I would kill all our sons."

When the queen was with child once more, the king had to go to war, but he left instructions that if she had a daughter, his sons were to be put to death. "Fly!" said the frightened queen to her sons. "If I give birth to a son, I will raise a white flag and you can come back. But if I bear a daughter, I will raise a red flag and you must stay away!" And her sons ran away.

One morning they saw a red flag flying, so they sadly built themselves a hut in the jungle.

As their sister grew, she often asked about the twelve chests of clothes in her mother's house, but her mother would not tell her who they belonged to.

At last the girl could bear it no longer. She picked up a revolver and told her mother, "The first bullet is for you, and the second is for me if you won't explain the mystery of these chests." So her mother told her about her twelve brothers, and her father's terrible oath.

The girl comes upon her brothers' hut

At gunpoint, a mother tells her daughter about her missing brothers

The girl took her father's ring and went to look for her brothers. She walked a long way, until she happened upon her brothers' hut.

Now the brothers had sworn to kill any woman who came to their hut, because it was for the sake of a woman that they had been exiled. For that reason, one of them always stayed behind when the others went hunting. When he saw a girl approaching, he menacingly asked her who she was and what she wanted. She showed him her father's ring, and he knew she must be his sister.

"Hide," he said, "or my brothers will kill you!"

When he cooked supper that night, he accidentally laid plates for thirteen, not twelve, so his brothers guessed someone else was there.

The girl had to show herself; but when they saw her ring, they forgave everything and begged her to stay with them.

The next day, the sister cooked for her brothers. They had a rose tree with twelve buds on it, and she picked the buds and laid one on each plate. But when the brothers came home and sat down to eat, they changed into twelve macaws and flew away. The girl resolved to search for them and vowed that, until she found them, she would not speak a single word to anyone.

A prince falls in love with the silent girl and takes her home

She cooks a meal for her brothers, but they turn into macaws and fly away

The girl

She vows not to speak until she finds them

Her silence angers the prince's sisters, who condemn her to death as an evil spirit

She wandered until her clothes were in tatters. A prince found her, fell in love, and took her home to be his bride, but she would not speak. The prince's sisters said, "She does not speak because she is an evil spirit." The girl would not speak to deny the charge and was condemned to death.

Just as she was about to die and the prince was begging her to speak to save herself, twelve macaws flew out of the jungle. The girl heard them calling "raf-raf!" and spoke at last. "Here are my brothers, come to save me!" she cried. The macaws turned back into her twelve brothers and the girl and the prince were married.

Her brothers arrive to save her from death

A Whale's Soul & Its Burning Heart

The raven flies straight into the whale's mouth

———— ———— ————

ALASKAN TALE
This haunting story shows the Inuits' respect for the beauty and fragility of life in the harsh Arctic. It was told to the Danish/Inuit ethnologist Knud Rasmussen by Pamik, an Inuit from the the Utokok River region in Alaska.

HUNTING TO SURVIVE
In the freezing seas off the Greenland coast, an Inuit hunter throws a spear at a narwhal. Whale meat and other products are vital to the traditional Inuit way of life. Anyone killing a whale – especially one as large as the whale in this tale – would be admired and respected.

THERE WAS ONCE a stupid and self-important raven who flew far, far out to sea. It flew and flew, until at last it grew tired. It looked for somewhere to rest, but there was no land. The raven grew so tired it barely had the strength to flap its wings. Just as it was about to sink into the ocean, a great whale came up to the surface, and the raven flew straight into its mouth.

As it tumbled down the whale's throat, the raven thought it must surely die. But then it found itself in a house, a neat, snug house full of light and warmth. It was a whalebone house, built and furnished like the houses of men. On a bed sat a young woman tending a glowing lantern. She welcomed the raven, saying, "Make yourself at home. But please, never touch my lantern." The raven promised never to meddle with the lantern.

The young woman seemed very restless. She was always getting up and going out the door, then coming back in again.

"What's the matter?" asked the raven.

"Nothing," said the girl. "It is just life. Life and breath."

The raven promises not to touch the girl's lantern

The raven grew curious about the girl and the lantern. So when she next slipped from the room, the raven touched the lantern's candle. Immediately the girl fell headfirst through the door and lay in a dead faint. The candle in the lantern went out.

It was too late for the raven to be sorry. The damage was done. The bright warm house was gone, and the raven was left in darkness, with the smell of the whale's fat and the whale's blood. It tried to find its way out of the whale's belly, but just kept going in circles, getting hotter and hotter and rubbing all its feathers off. The feathers swirled around so that the raven almost choked to death.

The girl was the whale's soul, and she slipped out through the door into the air whenever the whale drew breath. Her heart was the lantern with its steady flame. When the raven touched the lantern, it snuffed out the whale's heart's flame. Now the whale was dead, and the raven was trapped in its belly.

The raven fought for life in the blood and darkness, and at last it managed to haul itself out of the whale's mouth. Exhausted, it sat slumped on the floating carcass – a naked raven, smeared with grease and filth, on the back of a dead whale.

Eventually a storm came up and drove it toward land. The people saw the whale's carcass and rowed out in their kayaks to bring it to land. The raven saw them coming and changed itself into a man – a battered, ugly, little man standing on a dead whale.

The raven did not say, "I meddled with a beauty I could not understand and destroyed it."

STORM LANTERN
The Inuit used whale oil to fuel lamps and to make candles. In this story, the candle flame, symbolizing the whale's heart, is protected from sudden drafts by a storm lantern.

The meddling raven touches the lantern, its light goes out, and the girl faints away

When people come to see the whale's carcass, they meet an ugly little man shouting in triumph

Instead it crowed, "I killed the whale! I killed the whale!"
And the raven became a big man among men.

Beauty & the Beast

CLASSIC TALE
Although many
versions of "Beauty and
the Beast" have been
written down or told by
word of mouth, the one
that remains best
known – and which
forms the basis of this
retelling – is the classic
text of Madame Jeanne-
Marie de Beaumont
(above), first published
in 1756.

A DOG'S WIFE
"Beast-marriage" stories
are found all over the
world – the prince may
be a ram, a pig, a snake,
even a crocodile.
In an English version,
the beastly future
bridegroom is "a great,
foul, small-tooth dog."
In Kentucky, a similar
story is called "The Girl
that Married a Flop-
Eared Hound-Dog."

ONCE THERE LIVED a rich merchant who had three sons and three daughters. He was especially fond of the youngest girl. She was so pretty that, when she was small, everyone called her "Little Beauty," and the name stuck. Her older sisters, who weren't quite so attractive either in looks or character, couldn't help being jealous.

Beauty's haughty sisters had plenty of suitors but declared that they wouldn't dream of marrying anyone who wasn't a duke or a count. Beauty just said to anyone who proposed to her, "Thank you, but I'm too young to marry, and besides, I couldn't leave my father."

One day the merchant's ship was lost at sea and with it his fortune. All he had left was a cottage in the country. He sadly told his children that they would all have to move there and work the land. Although Beauty wasn't used to such hard work, she said, "Of course, father. Why, I'm sure it will be fun." But her sisters moaned about having to give up their fine dresses and high-and-mighty ways. Poor Beauty ended up doing all the work, while her sisters did nothing but complain about being stuck in the boring country.

A year later, the merchant heard that his ship, of which

Beauty does all the work while her sisters complain of being bored

he had given up all hope, had arrived safely in port after all, laden with goods. When he went to see about selling the cargo, he asked the girls what they would like best as a present on his return. The two eldest clamored for jewels, dresses, and expensive trinkets. Beauty, who realized the sale of the cargo would scarcely buy everything her sisters wanted, kept quiet.

"Don't you want anything, Beauty?" asked her father.

"Just a rose," she replied gently.

He came upon the gates to a great palace

When the merchant reached the port, however, he found that the cargo had already been sold to pay off his debts, and he was as poor as ever. Very downhearted, he turned back the way he had come. The only thing that cheered him up was the thought of seeing his family again.

He was some way from home when a snowstorm blew up and he became lost in a forest. The wind howled and the snow swirled and he couldn't tell left from right or up from down. But just when he thought he must surely die, he came upon the gates to a great palace. He urged his poor horse on and reached the safety of the courtyard. Everything was prepared in the stable, but there were no other horses there, and no stable-lads either.

The merchant entered the palace. Still there was no one to be seen. But he found a table set with roast chicken and wine, so he helped himself to supper. Then he went upstairs, found a bed, and, exhausted, fell asleep.

In the morning, he found a fine suit of clothes laid out for him to replace his weatherstained ones. Downstairs, breakfast had been laid. "This must be the house of some good fairy, who has taken pity on me," he mused.

Outside, the snow had melted, and beautiful flowers were blooming in the garden. The merchant remembered his promise to Beauty and went outside to pick a rose. As soon as he had done so, he heard a terrible roaring that made him go weak at the knees. He looked up. A hideous, snarling creature, half man, half beast, towered over him.

CASTLE IN THE WOOD
The beast's palace could well have looked like this castle in Saumur, France, which was designed to keep out unwelcome visitors.

The merchant is caught stealing a rose by the furious, roaring Beast

BEAUTY'S ROSE
The rose that may have
caught the merchant's
eye might have been
similar to *Rosa centifolia*,
rose of a hundred petals,
which was much
admired in 18th-century
France. It was grown to
imitate a rose from
China that was so
popular it was copied
onto porcelain and silk
embroideries.

THE HARPSICHORD
Before the advent of the
piano, it was common
to find harpsichords in
French drawing rooms
of the 18th century. A
refined young lady
much like Beauty would
sit and play a stately air
by the popular
composers of the day,
such as François
Couperin or Jean-
Philippe Rameau.

"Ungrateful wretch!" it boomed. "I welcome you into my castle,
feed you and take care of you, and in return you steal my roses, which
I love more than anything in the world. You shall die for this!"

The merchant threw himself to his knees. "Forgive
me, sir, I beg you! I plucked only one rose, for my
daughter, who asked me for one."

"Don't call me sir. My name is Beast, and I
don't care who knows it. But now you tell me
you have a daughter, I've a mind to let you go.
On one condition. She must come here of her
own free will, to die in your place. Otherwise,
you must return yourself in three months."

Although the merchant had no intention
of sacrificing one of his daughters to the
Beast, he agreed, thinking, at least I'll be
able to hold them in my arms before I die.

The Beast sent him home with a chest of
gold coins, but a heavy heart. When he told
everything to his daughters, the older ones said,
"It's all Beauty's fault, asking for fol-de-rols like
roses instead of jewels and clothes."

*Beauty's sisters, with the
help of half an onion,
weep at her departure*

Beauty replied, "If it is my fault, I must mend it. I will go to the
Beast and beg his mercy."

Beauty's father tried to stop her from going, but she refused to be
persuaded. So they set out together for the Beast's palace. Beauty's
father and brothers were weeping, and even her sisters managed a tear
or two, with the help of an onion.

When Beauty and her father arrived at the palace, everything was as
before, except this time two places had been laid for dinner. "The
Beast must want to fatten me up before he eats me," thought Beauty

After they had eaten, they heard a growl and the Beast appeared.
The Beast asked her if she had come of her own free will.

"Yes," she said, in a trembling voice.

"Then you shall stay," the Beast replied. "But your father must go."
The merchant protested in vain. Beauty remained behind, alone.

Upstairs, she found a bedroom with "Beauty's Room" in gold on the
door. Inside there was everything she could desire, even a
harpsichord. "Surely the Beast wouldn't have gone to all this trouble
if he meant to eat me right away," she thought.

The Beast joined her at supper the following night and told her that as long as she stayed with him, she had only to ask for something and she should have it. "You are the mistress here," he said, "and I am the servant. Tell me, am I very ugly?"

Beauty enters her beautiful room

Beauty's father is expelled from the palace

At supper, the Beast asks Beauty to marry him

"Yes," said Beauty. "But you are also very kind."

"That's probably only because I'm so stupid," said the Beast.

"Not at all," said Beauty. "Really stupid people think they're very clever. You have a good heart, so you can't be stupid."

And the Beast replied, "In that case, Beauty, will you marry me?"

"No," said Beauty. "I will not."

LA BELLE ET LA BETE
This story has been dramatized many times, including as an opera by André Grétry, *Zémire et Azor*, and a 1991 Walt Disney cartoon. Perhaps the most atmospheric adaptation was the film *La Belle et la Bête*, (above), directed by Jean Cocteau in 1946. It starred Josette Day as Beauty and Jean Marais as the Beast.

FANCY DRESS
This 18th-century silk brocade dress has supports called paniers at the hips. It would have made a fine gift for a gentleman like the Beast to offer his lady.

After that, the Beast asked Beauty every evening if she would marry him, and every evening Beauty turned him down.

Otherwise they lived happily, but Beauty missed her father. She had learned from looking in a magic mirror that her brothers had joined the army, and that her two older sisters had married, so her father was all alone. She begged the Beast to let her visit him for just a week, and promised to return.

"Make sure you do," said the Beast, "or I shall die of sorrow."

In the magic mirror Beauty sees her father looking lonely and ill

Beauty's sisters envy her beautiful clothes and jewels and plot her downfall

When Beauty got home, she found her father lying in bed. He had never recovered from the shame of leaving her with the Beast.

"Father, there's no need to be sad," she said. "The Beast is good and kind. Why, just look at the beautiful dress I am wearing; that is just one of his gifts." So Beauty's father began to cheer up. But when her envious sisters, who had made poor marriages, saw how grand Beauty had become, they were beside themselves with spite. They decided to make the Beast so angry he would eat her after all. They begged and pleaded until Beauty agreed to delay her return by one more week.

On the tenth night, Beauty dreamed she was in the Beast's garden and he was lying dead at her feet. She awoke shaking. She realized how fond she had grown of him, and how much she missed him.

She went straight back to the Beast's palace, but he was nowhere to be found. She ran into the garden, and there, just like in her dream, was the Beast, lying on the grass. She threw herself down beside him, hugging him and begging him to wake. She bathed his forehead in her tears. The Beast opened his eyes.

"You are too late," he croaked. "I am dying."

"Don't die!" said Beauty. "I want to marry you!"

CUPID AND PSYCHE
This tale shows the influence of the Roman story of Cupid and Psyche, told by the poet Apuleius in the 2nd century. The beautiful Psyche is forced by the gods to marry a monster, who is really Cupid, god of love, in disguise. This 19th-century painting of the moment Cupid and Psyche meet face to face is by British artist Sir Edward Burne-Jones.

The envious sisters are turned to stone

Beauty finds the Beast lying in his garden, dying

As she spoke, the palace exploded with light and music. The Beast was gone, and in his place was a handsome young prince.

"Beast, where are you?" called the anxious Beauty.

"Here I am," said the prince. "It was me all along, under a cruel spell. I had to find a girl who would love me for my good heart, not for my looks, or intelligence, or wealth. And now I have found you, I will never lose you again."

Beauty and the Beast were married and lived happily ever after. As for Beauty's sisters, the fairy who had enchanted the Beast turned them into statues to stand on either side of the palace doors. It was their punishment to see Beauty's happiness, and be unable to spoil it.

SAD ENDING
In a Portuguese version of the story, Beauty is tricked by her sisters and fails to return to the Beast in time. Beauty rushes back to the castle, but finds the Beast dead. She is so upset she pines away, and her jealous sisters are condemned to a life of poverty.

Three Magic Oranges

HOT JUNGLES
In Costa Rica's tropical jungles, where this story is set, the daytime temperature is 100° F (38° C) – hot enough to make anyone thirsty!

ONCE UPON A TIME an old king thought it high time his son was married. He invited princesses from far and near to a feast, but the prince didn't like any of them.

The king declared that his son had better find *himself* a wife. So the prince mounted his horse and rode off. Before long he reached a forest, at the edge of which was an orange tree with three golden oranges. He picked the oranges and went on his way.

It was a hot day, and the prince felt thirsty. He pulled out his knife and cut open the first orange. Wonder of wonders! From it sprang a beautiful maiden with eyes the color of the sky and hair the color of the sun. "Give me a drink of water, I beg you," she pleaded. But the prince had no water to give her, and the girl vanished.

The third time, the prince has water to give the girl and breaks a witch's spell

The prince finds three oranges

Twice he cuts open an orange; each time a maiden appears, begs for water, then vanishes

SAME GIRL
Though the girls in this tale look different, they are really the same person – there is only one enchanted maiden, not three.

The sun beat down and the prince cut open the second orange. Wonder of wonders! From it sprang a maiden with eyes the color of a forest pool and hair the color of a red hibiscus. She also begged him for water he did not have. Then she vanished.

At last the prince came to a spring and drank his fill. Feeling hungry, he cut open the third orange. Wonder of wonders! From it sprang a maiden with eyes and hair black as a raven's wing and a face as white as a jasmine flower. "Give me water, I beg you," she pleaded. He scooped some up for

The witch thrusts a pin into the girl's head – turning her into a dove

her to drink. And so the spell was broken, for a witch had imprisoned her in the magic oranges.

The prince and the girl were married and before long they became king and queen. But the witch discovered that the girl had been set free and went up to the palace, crying out, "Hairpins! Who'll buy my fine hairpins?"

The queen asked the old woman to come in. The witch took out a hairpin topped with a pearl. "Let me fix this in your hair," she said. The queen bowed down and the witch thrust the pin into her head. She was turned into a white dove, which flew away into the

forest where the young king was hunting.

The king caught the dove as a present for his wife. To his dismay, when he came home, she was nowhere to be seen.

Months passed. His only comfort was the white dove, a reminder of his lost love. One day, as he stroked the bird's head, he felt the pearl head of a pin. Who could have been so cruel? He pulled the pin out and – wonder of wonders! There stood his beautiful queen.

The king ordered his men to bring the witch to the palace, but there was no need. That day her hut caught fire and she was burned to death. The last anyone saw of her was a plume of smoke, blowing over the treetops.

The dove is the prince's only comfort for the loss of his true love

AROUND THE WORLD
This story is truly international, being popular in Europe, India, and North and South America. It also inspired the Russian composer Sergei Prokofiev (1891–1953) to compose the opera *The Love for Three Oranges* (above), first performed in 1921.

One day he finds a pin in the dove's head, pulls it out, and his lost wife appears again

The furious witch accidentally burns herself to death

Urashima & the Turtle

STRANGE BUT TRUE?
This bronze statuette shows Urashima seated on a turtle, a symbol of long life. The tale first appeared in the *Nihon Shoki* ("Chronicles of Japan"), completed in AD 720. According to the chronicle, the climax of the story actually took place – in Urashima's home village of Midzu no Ye (Ejima) in southwestern Japan, in AD 477.

TIME SLIP
In folktales, days spent in fairyland are often the equivalent of years in the real world. When the Irish hero Oisin (pronounced "Isheen") wishes to leave *tir nan-Og*, the magical Land of Youth, to visit his home, his fairy wife lets him go on a white horse, but warns him never to get down from its back. He falls from the horse – and at once becomes an old man.

LONG AGO THERE LIVED a fisherman named Urashima. He lived at home with his mother, for he was unmarried. When she urged him to find a bride he answered, "I can only catch enough fish to feed two, so while you are alive I will not marry."

One day all he caught was a little turtle. "You will scarcely make a mouthful for mother and a mouthful for me," he said.

The turtle replied, "In that case, set me free! If you show me mercy, I will show you gratitude." Kind-hearted Urashima set the turtle free.

Several years later, when Urashima was out fishing as usual, a storm swept through the bay and capsized his boat. Like so many fishermen, he could not swim, and he seemed sure to drown. But as he splashed and spluttered, a huge turtle swam up from the depths. "I am the turtle whose life you once saved," it said. "Climb on my back."

The turtle did not take Urashima to the shore – it plunged down, down to Ryugu, the dragon king's palace at the bottom of the sea. "I am maid-in-waiting to the Dragon Princess Otohime," the turtle said. "She wishes to thank you herself for saving my life."

One day, all Urashima catches is a little turtle

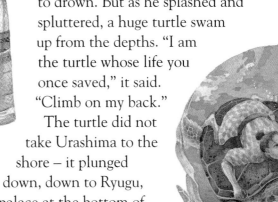

The giant turtle takes Urashima down to the bottom of the sea

As soon as they set eyes on each other, Urashima and the princess fell in love. She begged him to stay, telling him, "In this kingdom you will never grow old."

Three years passed and Urashima and the princess were very happy. Just one thing spoiled Urashima's contentment – worry about his mother. One day he asked Princess Otohime if he could visit her.

"If you go," she replied sadly, "you will not return." Urashima pleaded and at last she gave in. She placed a small casket in his hand,

saying, "Keep this safe, and never open it. If you do this, the turtle will meet you at the seashore and bring you back to me."

Urashima promised not to open the box. He seated himself on the turtle's back and the creature took him back to the beach he knew so well. But everything had changed. As he walked through his village, Urashima could not see anyone or anything he recognized. Where his home had been, only the stone washbasin and the garden steps remained. After a while he asked an old man if he had ever heard of a fisherman named Urashima.

"Don't you know the legend?" the old man replied. "It's said that Urashima lived in this village three hundred years ago, but he went down to the dragon kingdom under the sea and never came back."

"What happened to his mother?" asked Urashima.

"She died the day he left," the old man replied.

ISLES OF THE DRAGON
The Japanese word for palace of the dragon king is *ryugu* or *ryukyu* – the same as the name given to a long chain of islands running southwest from the Japanese coast across the East China Sea. Perhaps the beautiful Ryukyu Islands, the "palaces" of Li, mythical dragon ruler of the deep, were the setting for Urashima's love affair with Li's daughter, the dragon princess.

Urashima opens the box – and his body crumbles to dust

The dragon king's palace — Princess Otohime — Urashima

Sad that Urashima must leave her, the princess gives him a box, which he promises not to open

A PARTING GIFT
Since Japanese kimonos had no pockets, little boxes, tucked into a sash (*obi*) worn around the waist, were often used for carrying small items. This jewel box, inlaid with mother of pearl, dates from the 12th century AD.

Urashima could not believe his ears. "I am Urashima," he cried, "and I've only been away three years, not three hundred!"

He took out the box, saying, "Look, this was a parting gift from the dragon princess." In his haste, he forgot the dragon princess's warning, and opened the box. There was nothing in it but a puff of smoke. And as the smoke escaped, the weight of years fell on Urashima. His skin wrinkled, his legs gave way, and his body crumbled to dust.

Why the Sea Moans

ONCE UPON A TIME there was a queen who had been married for a long time but had never had a child. She prayed, "Please God, let me give birth, if only to a snake!" God heard her prayer and she gave birth to a baby daughter. Around the child's neck, a snake was tightly coiled.

The princess was named Maria, and she made a friend of the snake, whose name was Dona Labismina. They used to walk along the seashore and the snake would leave Maria's neck and play in the waves; but if Labismina did not soon return and curl around her neck again, the princess would start to cry.

One day the snake went into the sea and did not come back. But she told Maria that if she was ever in danger, she should call for her.

Some years later, the queen of a rich neighboring kingdom fell ill. On her deathbed, she took a ring from her finger and gave it to her husband, the king. "If you ever marry again," she whispered, marry a princess whose finger fits this ring – not too slack and not too tight." With these words, she died.

The king, an old, ugly, evil-tempered man used to getting his own way, at once resolved to marry again. He sent the ring to all the princesses of all the kingdoms: but the ring didn't fit any of them.

At last only Princess Maria had not tried the ring. The old king called on her and roughly put the ring on her finger. To Maria's horror – but to her parents' delight, since the vile old king was immensely rich – it fit just right. The king told Maria he would marry her without delay.

Maria was so unhappy she cried all the time. She went to the seashore and called for Labismina, and the snake came. Maria told her what was wrong, and the snake said, "Don't worry. Tell the king you will only marry him if he gives you a dress the color of the field, with all its flowers."

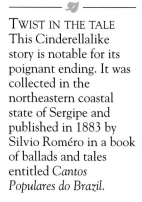

The queen's prayers are answered and she has a daughter, Maria, around whose neck coils a snake, Dona Labismina

Maria's parents

The king

The ring fits Maria's slender finger

TWIST IN THE TALE
This Cinderellalike story is notable for its poignant ending. It was collected in the northeastern coastal state of Sergipe and published in 1883 by Silvio Roméro in a book of ballads and tales entitled *Cantos Populares do Brasil*.

The princess did as she was told, and the king was very annoyed. But so struck by her beauty was he that he told her he would search for such a dress. And, though it took him a long time, he found one.

Then the princess went to Labismina, who told her, "Tell him that you will only marry him if he gives you a dress the color of the sea, with all its fish."

The princess did so, and the king was even more vexed than before. But though it took him a long time, at last he found one.

The princess went again to Labismina, who told her, "Tell him that you will only marry him if he gives you a dress the color of the sky, with all its stars."

She did so, and, though the king was angrier than anyone had ever seen him, he promised to look for one. He took even longer than before, but at last he found just such a dress.

ON THE SHORE
Sergipe is Brazil's smallest state. The beaches near its capital, Aracajú, may have helped inspire the seashore setting of parts of this tale.

Labismina

Fearing she will have to marry the ugly old king, Maria sails away, taking her three beautiful dresses with her

LUSCIOUS BLOOM
A magical dress featuring all the country's flowers would feature many spectacular blooms, such as this orchid from central Brazil.

The desperate princess ran to the sea and boarded a ship, which Labismina had got ready. Labismina said, "Sail away in this ship, land wherever it takes you, and you will marry the prince of that kingdom. On your wedding day, come to the sea, and call my name three times. Then I will be disenchanted, and I will be a princess, too."

Maria's boat lands on a deserted beach and she sets off to find work

The palace

She is put in charge of the king's hens

When a festival is held, Dona Labismina makes sure that Maria makes a big impression

Maria

The prince

The prince sees Maria for the first time

The prince sees Maria for the second time

Maria, in her sea-colored dress

He falls deeply in love, but no one knows who the mysterious girl is

HARD TIMES
Northeastern Brazil, from where this story comes, has many very poor areas. Only in fairy tales would Maria have found work so easy to come by.

PARTY DRESS
The wonderful dresses Maria wears to the fiesta are typical of the beautiful prints worn by many of the women of northeastern Brazil.

So Maria left, and where her ship stopped she went ashore. She had nothing to live on, so she went to the palace and begged for a job – she was put in charge of the king's hens.

After a while, there was a three-day festival in the town. Everyone in the palace went, except Maria, who was told to watch the hens. But, after everyone had gone, she put on her dress the color of the field, with all its flowers, asked Labismina for a beautiful carriage, and went to the festival herself.

Everyone gasped and gaped to see such a pretty girl, for no one recognized her. The prince, the king and queen's son, fell head over heels in love. But Maria left before the festivities ended, and by the time the royal family had returned to the palace, she was back in her old poultry-maid's gown. She heard the prince say, "Mother, did you see that lovely girl at the festival? I wish I could marry her! Don't you think she looked rather like our poultry maid?"

"That ragged, dirty creature?" replied the queen.

Later the prince went up to Maria and said, "Poultry maid, at the festival today I saw a girl who looked rather like you!"

"Oh! Prince, don't make fun of me," answered Maria.

The next day there were more festivities and Maria went again, wearing her dress the color of the sea, with all its fish.

On her wedding day, Maria is so very happy…

The prince fell even deeper in love, but nobody could tell him her name. On the third day, Maria wore her dress the color of the sky, with all its stars. The prince gave her a jewel on the church steps. When he returned to the palace, the love-sick prince took to his bed and refused to touch any food. Finally the queen asked the poultry maid to make him some broth.

FIESTA!
In Brazil, festivals such as Carnival, with traditional music and samba dancing, often go on for several days. In smaller towns they are often held in the main square in front of the church.

———— 🍃 ————

SOUND OF THE SEA
In a later version of this story by Elsie Spicer Ellis, published in 1917, Maria is given the name Dionysia. At the end, Labismina reproaches the forgetful princess by calling "Dionysia, Dionysia," a sound resembling waves breaking on a beach.

The prince gives his love a jewel, which he later finds in some broth made by the poultry maid

Maria sent some to the prince, and placed the jewel he had given her in the bowl. When the prince stirred the broth, he found the jewel. He leaped out of bed crying, "I'm cured! I'm going to marry the poultry maid!"

The queen sent for Maria, who arrived wearing her dress the color of the sky. Maria and the prince were married that very day.

Carried away by her own happiness, Maria forgot to go down to the seashore and call three times for her faithful Dona Labismina. So Labismina has never been freed from her enchantment.

And that is why the sea moans.

…that she forgets all about her faithful Dona Labismina

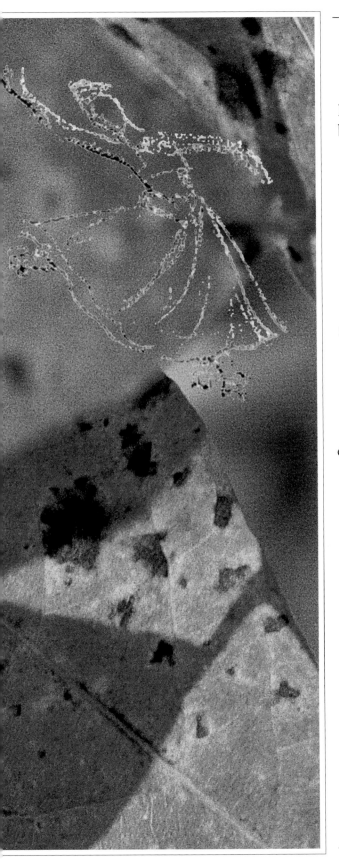

Riches & Rags

Fairy tales were originally told and listened to by poor people, and so it is not surprising that so many feature poor heroes hoping to make their fortunes. Sometimes they strike it rich through pure luck, like the fortune-teller Cricket, or by accidentally making a princess laugh, like Lazy Jack; sometimes they win through wit, like the heroine of "The Poor Girl Who Became Queen," or sly cleverness, like the Ash Lad in "That's a Lie!" More often, however, it is goodness, bravery, or fidelity that is eventually rewarded, usually by magic, as in "The Wonderful Brocade." Of course, as the drunken old skipper of "Easy Come, Easy Go" demonstrates, a chest full of money can be lost just as quickly as it can be won, while the grasping Fisherman's Wife emphasizes that even the best run of good luck can be pushed too far.

The Fisherman's Wife asks for too much and she and her husband find themselves back in their pigsty

Rumpelstiltskin

TALE SPINNING
The spinning and sewing rooms of castles and houses were storytelling centers. The work, done by women, was dull, and stories helped pass the time. So it is not surprising that so many tales mention spindles, spinning wheels, needles, and sewing.

FOOLS' GOLD
This 16th-century engraving shows alchemists at work, trying to change "base" material – perhaps lead or dung – into pure gold. Many noblemen employed alchemists in the vain hope of becoming rich. If only Rumpelstiltskin had been around to help!

A POOR MILLER ONCE boasted that his daughter could spin straw into gold. His wild words came to the ears of the king, who ordered the girl be brought to the palace. He shut her in a room filled with straw and said, "Spin this straw into gold by morning, or I will have you put to death."

The poor girl burst into tears. Suddenly the door opened and a little man entered. "Why are you crying?" he asked.

"Because I have to spin this straw into gold," she sobbed. "And I can't do it!"

"What will you give me if I do it for you?"

"My necklace," said the miller's daughter eagerly.

The little man took her necklace and sat down at the spinning wheel… By morning all the reels were full of gold. When the king saw this, his heart filled with greed. He shut the miller's daughter in a bigger room filled with straw, and commanded her to spin all of it into gold before morning, if she valued her life.

The miller

The king orders the miller's daughter to spin straw into gold

A strange little man appears who offers to do the work for the girl if she gives him her necklace

Once again the girl burst into tears, and the little man appeared and asked, "What will you give me if I do it for you?"

"My ring," she replied.

The little man took her ring and sat down at the spinning wheel…

The king's heart leaped when he saw all the gold. He shut the girl in an even bigger room filled with straw and told her: "If you can spin all this straw into gold, I will make you my wife. But if you fail, you will be put to death."

Once more the little man came to the miller's daughter and asked her, "What will you give me if I do it for you?"

"I have nothing left to give," she sobbed.

The little man said, "Promise me that if you become queen, you will give me your first child, and I will spin the straw into gold."

The miller's daughter had no choice but to agree.

When, next morning, the king saw all the gold, he thought, "I'll never find a better wife!" So the miller's daughter became his queen.

THE CHANGELING
"A living soul is more precious than riches," says Rumpelstiltskin. It was once believed that fairies snatched away children. Sometimes a gloomy fairy child, called a changeling, would be left in the human child's place. If the changeling could be made to laugh, the fairies would return the stolen child.

The little man sets to work and fills reel after reel with gold thread. In the morning, the king is delighted

A year later the queen gave birth to a fine boy. As she nursed him, she never gave a thought to the little man. But one morning, there he was, saying, "Give me what you promised."

The king resolves to make the girl his queen

"When I made that promise, I was poor, and had nothing else to give you," the queen replied. "But now I can make you rich beyond your dreams. What use is my baby to you?"

"A living soul is more precious than riches," replied the little man. "I will have what I was promised."

"Give me what you promised," says the little man

53

GNOME NAMES
Rumpelstiltskin goes by many names in many parts of the world, including Panczimanczi (Hungary), Purzinigele (Austria), Whuppity Stoorie (Scotland), Ricdin-Ricdon (France), Tom Tit Tot (England), Trit a Trot or Even Trot (Ireland), and Trwtyn-Tratyn (Wales).

The queen begged and beseeched, and at last he said, "If in three days you can find out my name, you may keep your baby."

The queen lay awake all night thinking what the creature's name might be. When he came to her room the next morning she asked, "Is your name Caspar?"

"That is not my name," the little man replied.

"Melchior?"

"That is not my name."

"Balthazar?"

"That is not my name."

She tried every name she had ever heard of, but the answer was always, "That is not my name."

On the second day she sent her servant out to look for unusual names. She tried them all, but the little man always replied, "That is not my name."

On the third day the servant came back and said, "I have not been able to find a single new name. But as I was walking through the forest, I came to a high hill. There I saw a hut. Nearby a fire was burning and a little man was capering about, singing:

"Today I'll brew, tomorrow bake,
After that the child I'll take.
I'll brew today and bake tomorrow;
The poor queen's heart will break from sorrow.
For I know neither sin nor shame,
And Rumpelstiltskin is my name."

Next morning the little man asked the queen, "Your Majesty, what is my name?"

"Is it Tom?"

"That is not my name."

"Is it Dick?"

"That is not my name."

"Is it Harry?"

"That is not my name."

"Well, could it be Rumpelstiltskin?"

"The Devil told you that!" the little man screamed, and he stamped his right foot so hard that his whole leg sank into the ground. In a terrible fury, he took his left foot in both hands and pulled so hard he tore himself in two.

Rumpelstiltskin shouts out his name, unaware that one of the queen's servants is watching

CRICKET, THE FORTUNE-TELLER 🍂 Trinidadian

🍃 Cricket, the Fortune-Teller 🍃

A BUTLER, A MAID, AND A COOK once stole a ring from a king. The king longed to get it back and put up a notice that read, "Fortune-Teller Wanted."

A poor, hungry sailor named Cricket saw the notice and thought, "That's a way to get three meals a day." He went to the king and claimed he was a fortune-teller. The king told Cricket about the missing ring and begged him to use his powers to find it.

The next morning the butler brought Cricket breakfast. Cricket, who had thoughts only for his three meals, murmured, "Here's one!"

The guilty butler ran out. At midday the maid brought Cricket's lunch. Cricket, who was still very hungry, said, "Here's the second one." The maid left, shaking with fear.

At dinnertime the cook took Cricket his meal. Cricket said with satisfaction, "And here's the third!"

The cook flung himself at Cricket's feet. "Please, sir, have mercy! I'll give you fifty dollars if you don't tell the king we stole the ring!"

Cricket, who was a smart fellow when his stomach was full, laughed and said, "Give me the money and put the ring in the turkey's crop."

Then Cricket went to the king. "I know where your ring is," he announced. Come into the yard." When they got there, Cricket pointed at the turkey. "Cut off its head and look in its crop." When the turkey's head was cut off, there, sure enough, was the king's ring.

The king showered Cricket with gifts and threw a party so all his friends could meet his wonderful fortune-teller. "Ask him anything you want," said the king. "He's sure to know it."

One of the guests snatched up a cricket from the grass and, turning to Cricket, asked, "What do I have in my hands?"

Cricket had no idea. "Come on," said the king's friends.

"Th-that's t-t-too easy," he stammered.

"It better be," growled the king, "or the turkey won't be the only creature to lose its head today."

Cricket saw all was lost. "Poor Cricket," he sighed. The guest opened his hands and out jumped the cricket! The proud king made Cricket rich, and he had three meals a day for the rest of his life.

The wire bends,
And the story ends.

LUCKY GUESSES
This is a Trinidadian version of an international type of tale known as "Doctor Know-All," after a story by the Brothers Grimm. Stories of lucky guesses are popular all over the world – perhaps the poor people who told them could imagine making a fortune only by luck. Pictured above is a painting of Trinidad by Albert Goodwin.

Cricket

The king

The king's guest asks Cricket to tell him what he is holding in his hands

Mushkil Gusha

LAND OF THIRST
The setting for this story is the harsh desert of Iran, where little grows but thorn bushes and the occasional acacia tree.

GUARDIAN ANGEL
This fairy tale mingles folk belief with religion. Mushkil Gusha, is a mysterious, magical horseman similar in appearance to the warrior above. He brings great good fortune but expects loyalty in return.

ONCE UPON A TIME there lived a thorn-cutter, his wife, and daughter. One day they had no food left, so the thorn-cutter went into the desert to cut thorns to sell. He did not return until late in the evening, when he found the door of the house tight shut. He was so tired he fell asleep outside by his bundle of thorns. Next morning he went back into the desert, and that night, too, came home late and had to sleep outside the door.

On the third night he found the door tight shut again. By this time he was so wracked with hunger and thirst he sank to the ground. His head spinning, he thought he heard a man say, "Thorn-cutter, look! Out in the desert someone is giving away bread and rice!" The thorn-cutter staggered off into the desert, but could find no one, and when he got home, someone had set fire to his thorns and they were now just a heap of blackened twigs. He lay down and wept.

"What's the matter with you?" said a stranger. The thorn-cutter explained what had happened and the stranger said, "Say seven prayers, shut your eyes, and get up on my horse behind me."

The stranger rode to a place covered with pebbles of all shapes and sizes and said, "Pick up as many as you want."

The thorn-cutter didn't want any pebbles, but he filled his sack and pockets with them out of politeness.

Mushkil Gusha

The stranger tells him to pick up pebbles from the desert and take them home

A thorn-cutter encounters a stranger, Mushkil Gusha

The stranger took him home and said, "Say seven prayers, open your eyes, and dismount. Never forget Mushkil Gusha, Remover of Difficulties. Every Friday, tell the story of Mushkil Gusha, and give away dates and raisins in his memory."

The thorn-cutter promised faithfully to do so. Then he dismounted and knocked at his door. His wife and daughter let him in and he told them what had happened. After he had dumped the pebbles in a pile in the corner of the room, he went to bed.

Later that night, the thorn-cutter and his wife were awoken by a bright light, like pure moonlight, coming from the pile of pebbles. To their amazement, the pebbles had turned into precious stones!

The next day the thorn-cutter's wife took one of the gems to sell to a jeweler at the bazaar. The man said, "Ten gold coins." The wife, who had never owned anything worth so much as ten copper coins in her whole life, said, "Don't joke with me." So the jeweler offered her twenty gold coins. "Don't joke with me," said the wife. And so it went, till at last the exasperated wife said, "Just give me what it's worth!" The jeweler gave her a hundred gold coins.

After that, the thorn-cutter and his family wanted for nothing. When his daughter wanted to live in a palace, he built one for her, right opposite the palace of the princess.

SHOPPING CENTER
The bazaar, where the thorn-cutter's wife sells jewels, is a feature of Middle Eastern towns. It is a street of stalls and shops that sell everything from antiques to foodstuffs. Bargaining over prices is all part of the fun.

The man's wife and daughter

The man's wife sells a jewel at the bazaar

The princess

The pebbles turn into jewels

The thorn-cutter builds a palace opposite that of the princess

The thorn-cutter's daughter

The princess

While swimming, the princess hangs her necklace in a tree

The listener

When the necklace is lost, the thorn-cutter is blamed – until a man listens to the story of Mushkil Gusha

The next day, the necklace is found and the thorn-cutter freed, thanks to Mushkil Gusha

LUCKY STORY
When this story was recorded, in 1919, poor women used to fast on a Thursday and tell the story of Mushkil Gusha to a child on a Friday evening for good luck.

The princess wanted to know who had built such a splendid palace opposite hers. She asked the thorn-cutter's daughter to come on a picnic. They rode out to a lake, ate lunch, and went for a swim. The princess hung her necklace in the fork of a tree and the two girls played in the water all afternoon.

The next morning the princess missed her necklace. "The thorn-cutter's daughter must have stolen it," she said. All the thorn-cutter's possessions were confiscated and he was put in the stocks for everyone to mock.

"I haven't felt so miserable since the night Mushkil Gusha first came," he said to himself. Then he remembered with shame that it was a Friday evening, and that although he had promised to tell the story of Mushkil Gusha every Friday, he had never done so.

At his feet he noticed a copper coin. He held it out to passersby, crying "Take this coin to buy dates and raisins, and hear the tale of Mushkil Gusha, Remover of Difficulties." Nobody would stop.

At last a man came along who was visiting the bazaar to buy a shroud for his dying son. The man thought, there is nothing I can do for my son; it will be an act of kindness to hear this poor wretch's tale. So he bought some dates and raisins with the thorn-cutter's coin and listened to the story of Mushkil Gusha.

When the man got home, he discovered that his son had miraculously recovered. And the next morning a maidservant of the princess happened to go to the lake. Looking into the water, she saw the necklace. But when she put her hand in to grasp it, it vanished. Then she sneezed, and, raising her eyes, saw the necklace dangling in the tree, where it had been all the time. The thorn-cutter was freed and given back his riches and his palace.

May God, who granted the thorn-cutter's desire, grant also the desires of all mankind. Hail, Mushkil Gusha!

✿ I Ate the Loaf ✿

THREE MEN – two from the city and one from the country – set out on a pilgrimage to Mecca and agreed to share their food on the journey. But they didn't take enough with them, and at last all they had left was the flour to make one small loaf. As the loaf was baking, the men from the city fell to talking. "There isn't enough bread for three," said one.

"We need a plan," said the other. They put their heads together and then said to the countryman, "There isn't enough bread for all of us. So let us leave it till the morning, and the one who has had the most wonderful dream shall eat it." And the countryman agreed.

While the countryman bakes the loaf, the men from the city are scheming

However, when the two city dwellers were asleep, the crafty countryman got up and ate the loaf.

In the morning, the countryman woke first, but lay as if asleep. He overheard the city dwellers muttering to each other. "I'll say I dreamed that two angels took me off to heaven," one said.

"And I'll say I dreamed that two angels took me off to hell," said the other.

Then the countryman pretended to wake. "What! Are you back so soon?" he exclaimed.

"What do you mean?" asked the city dwellers.

"Why, I dreamed two angels came and took one of you to heaven and the other to hell. I didn't expect either of you to come back, so I ate the loaf!"

One man "dreams" of going to heaven

The other "dreams" of going to hell

The countryman "dreams" that both have died

HOLY CITY
Mecca, in Saudi Arabia, is the birthplace of the prophet Muhammad and the holiest city of Islam, the Muslim faith. Muslims, like the characters in this story, are expected to make a pilgrimage (*hajj*) to Mecca at least once in their lives. Pilgrims gather at the Great Mosque complex, pictured here.

———— ✿ ————

CROWD PLEASER
This tale comes from a medieval Latin collection by Petrus Alfonsus of Aragon. The story is also popular in both Arabic and in Jewish traditions, and is well known in many other cultures. It can easily be adapted so that the wily bread-eater is of the same background as the people listening to the story.

The Girl Who Combed Pearls

The girl's mother bequeaths her a magic towel and comb

Every time she uses the comb, pearls fall from her hair

Her sailor brother takes some of the pearls to show to the king of a faraway land

GOLDEN MOUTH
In other versions of this story, the girl has the gift of dropping gold or jewels from her mouth when she speaks. But from her jealous rival's mouth fall only toads.

THERE ONCE lived a woman who had a daughter and a son who was a sailor. One day the mother fell ill. She called her daughter to her and gasped, "I've nothing to give you but this towel and this comb. Use them and think of me." Then she died. From that day on the girl always dried herself with her mother's towel and combed her hair with her mother's comb. Each time she did so, pearls fell like tears from her hair and her skin. She told her brother, who declared, "I'll take these pearls on my next voyage and sell them."

He sailed to a faraway land and showed the pearls to the king. He also told him about his sister and her wonderful towel and comb.

"Not only do I want these pearls," the king exclaimed, "I want to see your sister, too. If what you say is true, I'll marry her. But if it's false, I'll put you to death."

The brother sailed home happily. His sister was so delighted she couldn't resist telling her witchy neighbor the news: "I'm going to be a queen!"

"Since you're going to be so grand," her neighbor replied, "you won't mind my daughter and me coming along, too."

On the voyage, the neighbor gave the girl poison and she fell down in a faint. Her heart was stilled; not a breath stirred in her body.

She was buried at sea by her brother, who wept bitterly.

"Without my beloved sister, we must turn back, or the king will have my head," he sighed.

"And lose a fortune?" snapped the neighbor. "Why not pretend my daughter is your sister? She can take the towel and the comb and the king need never know." Reluctantly, the brother agreed.

They reached port and went to the king's palace. The sailor presented the neighbor's daughter to the king, saying, "I have brought my sister to be your wife."

"First let me see her comb pearls from her hair," the king replied.

The neighbor's daughter took out the comb, but instead of pearls, showers of dandruff speckled the carpet. The furious king ordered the brother to be thrown into prison to await execution.

That day the palace cook went down to the sea to catch fish. On the shore lay a dead whale. As he approached, he heard a voice crying "Let me out!" He cut open the whale's belly – and out stepped a beautiful girl. She told the cook a strange story indeed. He didn't know what to think, so he hid her in an upstairs room at the palace. There she spent her time gazing sadly from a tiny window.

SAILING AWAY
This model of a 15th-century ship called a *caravel* recalls Portugal's seafaring past. Many brave men, like the heroine's brother in this tale, set off to find their fortunes along the coasts of Africa, Arabia, the Orient, and the spice islands of the East Indies.

The palace cook cuts open the dead whale's belly – and a beautiful girl crawls out

One day she saw her brother's dog, Cylindra. "How is my brother?" she called. "Waiting to die," the dog replied.

The girl confided in the cook, who told the king everything.

The next day he and the king hid and waited. They heard the girl ask, "Cylindra, how is my brother?" This time the dog replied, "He will die today."

Cylindra, the dog

From her window at the palace, the girl sees her brother's dog, and asks it for news of him

Then the king asked the girl to comb her hair with her mother's magic comb. When she did so, pearls cascaded onto the floor. The king married her and set her brother free.

The scheming neighbor and her daughter were killed in his place.

WHALE OF A TIME
Being swallowed by a whale is a fate the heroine of this story shares with the wooden puppet Pinocchio. Created by Italian Carlo Collodi in 1883, he is pictured here by Charles Folkard.

"That's a Lie!"

Lying contests are a
staple of folktales the
world over, but this
particular kind is
especially common in
Scandinavia. In
England, a story holds
that a certain village
held a lying contest. A
bishop, passing by,
scolded the competitors,
saying, "For my part, I
never told a lie in my
life." They immediately
gave him the prize!

CHEESE-MAKING
A Scandinavian woman
strains digestive juices
from a calf's stomach to
ferment milk into
cheese. Cheeses made
by traditional methods
were tiny in comparison
with those mentioned
by the fibbing hero and
heroine of this tale.

ONCE UPON A TIME a king had a daughter who was a terrible fibber. The king said that if any man could out-fib her and get her to say, "That's a lie!" that man could have her for his wife, and half the kingdom besides. Many young men came to try their luck, but their feeble stories just prompted the princess to wilder and wilder lies of her own.

At last there came three brothers, who all wanted to give it a try. The first went into the castle boasting and came out in a sulk; the second went in bragging and came out in a temper. The princess hadn't listened to a word they had said, just sat there spinning stories.

Finally the youngest brother, the Ash Lad, strolled into the magnificent castle yard. Presently the princess came.

"Not much of a place you've got here," the Ash Lad said to her.

"Well I bet you've nothing to match it," she snapped. "Why, when two shepherds stand at opposite ends of this yard and blow their ram's horn trumpets, one can't hear the other!"

"Oh, ours is far bigger," said the Ash-lad. "When we've sheared a sheep we just make it walk around the yard and by the time it gets back, it's ready to be sheared again!"

The Ash Lad and the princess are soon trading tall stories in the castle yard

"I dare say!" said the princess. "But at least you haven't got such a huge ox as ours. You can sit a man on each horn and they can't touch each other with a shepherd's crook!"

"That's nothing," said the Ash Lad. "If two men sit on *our* ox's horns and blow ram's horn trumpets, they can't hear one another!"

"I dare say," she said, frowning, "but you don't have as much milk as we do, I'm sure. We've so much, we milk our cows into great pails, empty them into huge tubs, and make cheeses as big as carts!"

"Do you?" replied the Ash Lad. "We milk our cows into great tubs, put the tubs in carts, empty them into great brewing vats, and make cheeses the size of houses. We used to have an old brown mare to tread the cheese while it was making, until she fell in and we lost her. But it was all right, because after we'd been eating that cheese for seven years, we found her inside it, alive and kicking. Her backbone was broken, but I took a fir sapling and made her a new backbone out of that, and then she was right as rain. Well, that sapling grew into a fine fir tree, and I climbed right up to heaven on it. And when I got there, I saw the Virgin Mary sitting and spinning the foam of the sea into pig's-bristle ropes. Just then, the fir tree broke, and I couldn't get down; so the Virgin Mary let me down by one of the ropes, and I slipped straight down into a fox's hole. Who should I find there but my mother and your father, cobbling shoes! Just as I stepped in, my mother gave your father such a box on the ear it made his whiskers curl."

"That's a lie!" said the princess. "My father never did any such thing!"

And that's how the Ash Lad won the princess for his wife, and half the kingdom besides.

The Ash Lad's mother gives the princess's father a bang on the ear

The Virgin Mary

The Ash Lad

The Ash Lad slips down the Virgin Mary's pig's-bristle rope and slips straight into a fox's hole

The Boat That Sailed on Land

With her magic wand, the old woman turns Jean's rags into sails

IMMIGRANT STORY
This story was collected in French patois from the Old Mines area of Missouri by Joseph Médard Carrière in 1934. The French-speaking residents are descended from immigrants that came from Acadia in Canada to old Louisiana in the 18th century. In Europe the tale is also known as "The Extraordinary Companions" and "Six Go Through the Whole World." In some versions the boat flies.

THERE WAS ONCE an old couple with three sons. The king proclaimed that whoever could make a boat that could sail on land could marry his daughter, so the eldest son set off for the forest to build his ship. There he met an old woman who asked what he was making. "Wooden plates, witch," he snapped.

"You are, too," said the old woman. And however hard he worked, all he made were wooden plates. The second brother rudely told the old woman he was making wooden spoons, and that was all *he* made. When the youngest brother, Jean, went to the forest, the old woman asked him the same question.

"I'm making a boat that can sail on land," he said politely.

"I wish you well," she answered, and wandered off.

Jean set to work. The old woman came by at sunset just as he was hammering in the last nail. "The boat is finished," he cried.

"But there are no sails," she said.

Jean didn't know where to find sails, but the old woman said, "Gather all the rags you can find and bring them to me tomorrow."

The next morning she turned the rags into glorious sails and Jean went sailing over land to the king's palace.

On the way he met a man lying by a dried-up spring.

The king's palace

"What are you doing?" asked Jean.

"I've drunk this spring dry and I'm waiting for it to fill," came the reply. "My name is Bold Drinker."

"Come and sail with me," said Jean.

Hoping to marry the princess, Jean sails his magic boat to the king's palace with his companions – Bold Drinker, Greedy Eater, Sharp Hearer, Fast Runner, and Great Blower

Soon they met a man who was licking stones.

"These stones used to be part of an oven, and you can still taste the bread," said the man. "My name is Greedy Eater."

"Come and sail with me," said Jean.

Then they met Great Blower, who was blowing right across the ocean to turn a windmill's sails, and Sharp Hearer, who was listening to corn growing, and Fast Runner, who was running races with rabbits. They all went with Jean to see the king.

The king was not eager to give his daughter to a raggedy young fellow like Jean. He said that first Jean must find a man who could drink his cellar dry. Bold Drinker emptied every barrel!

Then the king challenged Jean to find someone who could eat a feast laid for a hundred. Greedy Eater did so and still wasn't full!

Then Jean had to find someone who could race the princess to the spring and back. Fast Runner set off, and was halfway back before the princess had even reached the spring. So he lay down for a little rest. Jean said, "Where's he got to?" Sharp Hearer put his ear to the ground and said, "I can hear him snoring. He's fallen asleep and the princess has passed him."

RIVERBOAT QUEEN Steamboats still operate on the Mississippi River to this day. Now they only ferry tourists, but in the 19th century "Riverboat Queens" were a vital mode of transportation. Perhaps the big wheel helped inspire the amphibious boat of this story.

Bold Drinker

Greedy Eater

Sharp Hearer

Great Blower

Fast Runner

No challenge is too great for Jean's friends: Bold Drinker drinks the king's cellar dry; and Greedy Eater eats enough for a hundred!

Great Blower said, "Leave it to me." He blew the princess right back to the spring, and woke up Fast Runner.

Jean and the princess were married, and Bold Drinker, Greedy Eater, Fast Runner, Sharp Hearer, and Great Blower lived with them for the rest of their days.

If Jean wants to marry the princess, she must be defeated in a race: Sharp Hearer, Fast Runner, and Great Blower see to that!

Lazy Jack

SILVER COIN
Until the mid-17th
century, pennies were
made of silver, not
copper, so Jack's wage
of a penny a day would
have been reasonable.

*Lazy Jack drops his
penny in a stream*

*The jug of milk spills
in Jack's pocket*

A BOY NAMED Jack lived with his mother in a dreary village. They were very poor. The old woman earned a little money sewing and mending, but all Jack did was sit by the fire in winter and laze in the sun in summer. At last she told him, "Work for your porridge or you'll get none!"

So Jack hired himself to a farmer for a penny for the day. But on the way home Jack dropped the penny as he crossed a stream and lost it. "You stupid boy!" said his mother crossly when he told her what had happened. "You should have put it in your pocket."

"I'll do so next time," said Jack.

The next day Jack went to work for another farmer. This farmer gave him a pitcher of milk for pay, and Jack put the pitcher in his pocket as his mother had told him. But as he walked home the pitcher jiggled in his pocket and milk slopped everywhere. "You ninny!" said his mother. "You should have carried it on your head."

"I'll do so next time," said Jack.

*Jack's mother scolds
her ninny of a son*

WRONG AGAIN!
This tale of a simpleton
who always gets things
wrong has been widely
told, especially in
Europe. More than a
hundred versions have
been collected in
Ireland and Finland. It
has also been found in
Asia and Africa. This
version comes from
Yorkshire, England.

The next day Jack went to another farmer, who gave him a cream cheese for his day's work. Jack put the cheese on his head as his mother had told him. But by the time he got home the soft cheese had run all over his hair.

"You featherbrain!" said his mother. "You should have carried it in your hands."

"I'll do so next time," said Jack.

*The soft cheese runs
all over Jack's hair*

The next day Jack hired himself to a baker who paid him with a tomcat. Jack carried it carefully in his hands, but before he was halfway home the cat scratched so much that he had to let it go. "You dolt!" said his mother. "You should have tied it with a string and dragged it along after you."

"I'll do so next time," said Jack.

The next day Jack hired himself to a butcher who paid him with a leg of mutton. Jack tied the mutton with a string and dragged it after him. By the time he got home it was filthy with dust. "You halfwit!" said his mother. "You should have carried it on your shoulders."

The tomcat scratches so much that Jack has to let it go

Jack drags the leg of mutton behind him in the dust

"I'll do so next time," said Jack.

The next day Jack hired himself to another farmer, who gave him a donkey for his trouble. Now Jack was a strong lad, but even so he found it hard to lift the donkey onto his shoulders, and he huffed and puffed as he carried it.

On his way home Jack passed the mansion of a rich man whose beautiful daughter had never laughed. The rich man had promised that anyone who could make her laugh could marry her.

The rich man's daughter was looking glumly out the window when Jack trudged by with the

Jack trudges by with a donkey on his shoulders

donkey on his shoulders, its legs sticking up in the air. The rich man's daughter couldn't help herself. She hooted with laughter till people around and about came running to see what was the matter. She and Jack were married and they lived happily in the mansion with her father and Jack's mother, and Jack never had to go to work again.

THE LAUGHING BRIDE
A rich girl who has never laughed also appears in "The Golden Goose," by the Brothers Grimm. The hero, Dummling, finds a golden goose. Everyone who touches the goose (except Dummling) becomes stuck to it or each other. When the girl sees Dummling leading a weird procession, she bursts out laughing, and later becomes his bride.

When she sees Jack, the rich man's daughter hoots with laughter

Prince Nettles

FIT FOR A KING
Vajdahunyad Castle,
Budapest, would make a
suitably splendid home
for King Yellow
Hammer in this tale.

*T*HERE WAS ONCE a miller who was so proud he thought an egg should feel honored if he stepped on it. He had a fine mill, but he thought it wasn't good enough for him, so he set off to look for a better one.

He wandered over seven times seven countries, and at last came to a tumbledown mill on the banks of a river. It was covered in nettles, but the miller began to rebuild it. He worked until his clothes were rags. Then he waited in his marvelous mill for people to ask him to grind their flour. He waited and waited, but no one came.

One day some huntsmen were chasing a fox. The fox ran up to the miller, crying, "Hide me!" The miller threw an old sack over the fox, and when the hounds came sniffing after it he chased them off. The fox came out from under the sack and said, "Thank you. Now I'll do *you* a good turn. How would you like to get married?"

"But I've only these miserable rags to wear," sighed the miller. "How can I hope to win the hand of *any* girl?"

"I'll find you a bride," the fox said.

The fox traveled over seven times seven countries to the court of King Yellow Hammer. "Your majesty," declared the fox, "I am the ambassador of Prince Nettles. He wishes to marry your daughter

The fox takes a lump of gold to King Yellow Hammer and tells him that Prince Nettles, his master, wants to marry his daughter

A miller waits and waits, but no one wants him to grind their corn

One day the miller saves a fox from hunters

The king's daughter

and sends this gold as a token of esteem. The prince is sorry to send you such a great lump of gold, but it's the smallest piece he has."

"Tell Prince Nettles we can't wait to see him," said the king.

So the fox went back to the miller and said, "Remember, you are Prince Nettles from now on. Come with me, and you shall be married." When the castle of King Yellow Hammer came in sight, the fox said, "That is the home of your bride."

The fox told the miller to take off all his clothes and bathe in the river. Then he ran to King Yellow Hammer and said, "Your majesty, Prince Nettles set out in a carriage so overloaded with gold and jewels that it has toppled into the river and sunk. I have only just managed to rescue the prince naked from the water!"

So King Yellow Hammer sent servants with fine clothes and a carriage to collect Prince Nettles, and after a month the miller and the king's daughter were married. Then the king's daughter said, "My love, take me home to your own castle."

The miller was worried at this, but the fox said, "Leave it to me."

They traveled home through the rich lands of Vasfogu Baba the witch, and everywhere they went, the fox had been before them, bribing the peasants to say that the land belonged to Prince Nettles. Meanwhile the fox visited Vasfogu Baba's castle.

"Tell me why I should not crush your bones as small as poppyseed," said the witch.

"Because the French army is coming!" the fox cried. "We must all hide. Come, I know a place where they will never find you."

The witch went with the fox to a bottomless lake. He pushed her in and she is probably still falling through its black, endless waters. Then the fox returned to the miller and declared, "You were born under a lucky star, for you are the sole heir of Vasfogu Baba, the witch."

And Prince Nettles, his bride, and the fox lived happily ever after.

HELPFUL CAT
This story is similar to the tale of "Puss in Boots" (illustrated here by a 19th-century postcard), which was first published by Frenchman Charles Perrault in 1697.

———— 🍃 ————

ON THE DUNGHEAP
In longer versions, an ungrateful Prince Nettles orders the fox to be thrown on a dungheap. But the fox threatens to reveal his secret and the prince asks for forgiveness.

The king's carriage

The fox tricks the king into thinking that Prince Nettles has had an accident

The witch dives into the lake and Prince Nettles takes her castle

The Fly

ONCE THERE WAS a rich man who lent money to all the poor people in the area at unfairly high rates of interest.

One poor peasant was heavily in debt. So the rich man went to see if he had any valuable possessions to confiscate.

When the rich man got to the peasant's hut, he found the man's little son playing in the yard. "Are your parents at home?" he asked.

"No," said the boy. "My father has gone to cut living trees and plant dead ones, and my mother is at the market selling the wind and buying the moon."

The rich man cajoled the boy and threatened him, but he always answered in the same words. So finally the rich man said, "Look. If you will tell me what you mean, I will forget the debt they owe me, as heaven and earth are my witness."

"Heaven and earth cannot talk," said the boy. "Some living thing should be our witness."

The rich man pointed to a fly that had settled on the door frame. "That fly can be our witness," he said.

So the boy told him, "My father has gone to cut down bamboos and make a fence with them, and my mother has gone to sell fans to buy oil for our lamps."

The rich man laughed. "You are certainly a clever boy," he said.

But a few days later the rich man came back to demand his money. The boy said, "Father, you need not pay." But the rich man denied he had ever made such a promise.

So the case came before the local landowner. The rich man said that he had never *seen* the boy, let alone made him any promise, and the boy said that he had. "It's one person's word against another's," said the landowner. "I can't judge either way without a witness."

"But there was a witness," said the boy. "A fly heard every word."

"A fly!" said the landowner. "Are you making fun of me?"

"No," said the boy. "There was a fly – a big, fat one, sitting on this gentleman's nose."

"You little liar!" shouted the rich man. "It wasn't on my nose, it was on the door frame!"

"Nose or door frame, it doesn't make any difference," said the landowner. "You *did* make the promise, so the debt is paid."

The rich man says a fly can be the witness to the deal he makes with the boy

VILLAGE ATMOSPHERE
This detail from a 1958 painting by Vietnamese artist Nguyen Van Ty perfectly conveys the village atmosphere of this tale. The humbling of a rich bully is a popular theme all over the world.

☙ The Endless Tale ☙

ONCE UPON A TIME there was a king who had a very beautiful daughter. Now this king was very fond of stories, and he said that she should marry the man who could tell him an endless tale. Anyone who could not tell an endless tale would be beheaded.

Many rich young men tried to tell an endless tale, but one by one they ran out of story, and one by one they lost their heads. At length a poor man came to court and said he wanted to try his luck.

"By all means," said the king.

The poor man began his tale and this is what he said: "There was once a man who built a barn that covered many acres of land and reached almost to the sky. He built it so well that there was only one hole in the roof, through which a single locust might creep. Then he filled the barn full of corn to the very top. When he had filled the barn, a locust came through the hole in the top and fetched a single grain of corn."

Another locust came…

and another locust came…

and another locust came…

"You call that a story?" cried the king. But the poor man hadn't finished.

"And then," he said, "another locust came and fetched another grain of corn." And the man went on saying "another locust came and fetched another grain of corn" until the whole court was heartily sick and weary of it.

and another locust came…

and another…

Another locust came and another locust came and another locust came. The king had had enough. "Isn't this story ever going to end?"

"No, your majesty," said the poor man.

"In that case," said the king, "you had better marry my daughter."

And he did, and his beautiful bride made him promise never to tell his endless tale again.

NEVER-ENDING STORY
This version of "The Endless Tale" comes from Nottinghamshire, England. Similar stories have been found in many countries. In one from Japan, rats, not locusts, are counted. In another, from Italy, a shepherd carries sheep over a stream.

The poor man's endless tale proves to be truly endless .

Shoes That Were Danced to Pieces

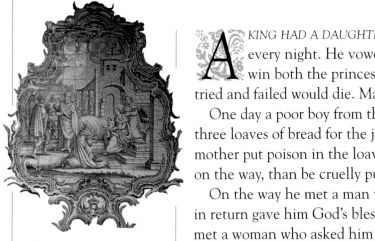

The princess

The princess takes
out six pairs of
shoes, watched by
the invisible boy

The boy's
shadow

She picks a flower
from a gold, copper,
and silver bush

RELIGIOUS DIFFERENCE
The Cape Verde Islands
were a Portuguese
territory and this story
reveals Portuguese
origins by its mention of
Catholic icons such as
St. Anthony and the
Virgin Mary (above).
The princess, who
dances with "devils,"
clings to pagan ways; for
this reason the boy
refuses to marry her.

HILLSIDE HOUSES
The city boy of this
story might well have
lived in a house like the
ones pictured above.

A KING HAD A DAUGHTER who wore out seven pairs of shoes every night. He vowed that whoever found out why would win both the princess and half his kingdom; but anyone who tried and failed would die. Many tried, but none succeeded.

One day a poor boy from the city asked his mother to bake him three loaves of bread for the journey and he set out to try his luck. His mother put poison in the loaves, thinking, "It's better he should die on the way, than be cruelly put to death by the king!"

On the way he met a man who asked him for one of the loaves and in return gave him God's blessing. That was St. Anthony. Then he met a woman who asked him for one of the loaves and in return gave him a coat of invisibility. That was the Virgin Mary. And lastly he met an old man who asked him for the last loaf and in return gave him a whip. That was God himself.

The king told him to sleep that night in a room next to the princess's. But instead he put on his coat of invisibility and tiptoed into the princess's room. He saw her take six spare pairs of shoes from a wardrobe and slip out of the room. He followed close behind as she stole down the main staircase and out of the palace.

First she came to a gold bush. "Good evening, gold bush," she said.

"Good evening, princess, and to your friend," the bush replied.

"I am alone," frowned the princess. She picked a flower and fastened it to her coat and the invisible boy did likewise. Next she came to a silver bush, then to a copper bush, and each time she claimed she was alone and each time first she, then her invisible companion, picked a flower.

The princess jumped on a white horse, which took her across a river. But the boy cracked his whip and was there before her.

They arrived at a palace full of devils dancing the night away. The princess danced a waltz and wore out her first pair of shoes; then she danced a mazurka, a reel, a strombolica, a contra-dance, a tango, and a sarabande, until all seven pairs of shoes were worn out. Then she rode on the white horse back to her father's palace. But the boy cracked his whip and was there before her. He rushed up to his room and lay down.

A white horse carries the princess across a river

🖋
DANCING GIRLS
Tales similar to this have been recorded all over Europe. The Brothers Grimm tell a version titled "The Twelve Dancing Princesses."

The boy follows her to a palace, where she wears out her shoes dancing with devils

The princess looked in, saw the boy asleep, and felt sure her secret was safe.

In the morning, the king asked his guest if he knew why his daughter wore out seven pairs of shoes every night. To his amazement, the boy replied, "Yes!" And to prove his tale he showed the king the flowers from the gold, silver, and copper bushes.

The king promised he could marry the princess.

"I'll marry no girl who dances with devils," the boy replied, "but give me half your kingdom, and me and my mother will be happy the rest of our days!"

The flowers prove the boy's story, but he throws them away – and the princess, too!

The Wonderful Brocade

FINE THREADS
The Chinese have excelled at brocade work – weaving raised designs onto cloth – since ancient times. This 19th-century example shows a phoenix on a robe belonging to Empress Dowager Tz'u-hsi.

CHINESE LOOM
Weaving in China began c.2500 BC. Weaving was done using both small hand looms and also large machines like the 19th-century one above.

O NCE UPON A TIME there lived an old widow with three sons. She supported her family by weaving brocades. The animals, birds, and flowers she wove almost seemed alive.

One day when she went to town to sell her work, she saw a wonderful picture in a shop. It showed a big house set in a lovely garden. Just looking at it made her feel happy. Instead of buying rice to eat, she bought the picture.

When she got home, she showed it to her sons. "Look at this beautiful place!" she said. "That's where we should live."

"Only in our dreams," said her eldest son.

"Or perhaps after we die," said her second son.

"If we can't live there, mother," said her youngest son, "why don't you copy the picture? While you're weaving, you'll feel as if you're there."

The widow buys a wonderful picture and decides to weave a copy of it for herself

So his mother took her brightest silk thread and started to weave the wonderful picture in brocade. Day after day she worked, determined to do her best work. Her first two sons were not at all pleased. "We're tired of gathering firewood to buy the family's rice," they grumbled. "Stop this foolishness. Make some brocades to sell!"

"Leave her alone," her youngest son said. "This picture means everything to her. If you're too tired to gather firewood, I'll do it."

The eldest comes upon a mysterious stone horse

So from then on the two boys lounged around all day while their young brother collected firewood and their mother wove.

She worked all day and all night. Weaving in the evening by the flickering fire made her old eyes hurt, but she never stopped. After a year, her tears fell like rain upon the cloth, and where they landed she wove a little river and a pond. After two years, blood fell from her

The widow finishes her brocade, but a breeze snatches it away

The youngest son

Her oldest sons do nothing while the youngest works to support the family

The widow begs her three sons to find her wonderful brocade

eyes onto the cloth, and where it landed she wove a red sun and many flowers. After three years, the brocade was finished.

How beautiful it was! The house had turquoise walls, red pillars, and blue tiles on the roof. There was a garden full of flowers, and in the middle of the garden was a pond full of fish. On one side was an orchard full of fruit and singing birds; on the other a vegetable plot just ready to harvest. Rice and corn grew tall in the fields. A sparkling stream ran past the house and a red sun shone above it.

Delighted with her work, the old woman took the brocade outside to admire it in the sunshine. Suddenly a fierce gust of wind snatched it away and the wonderful brocade disappeared into the sky.

"Find my brocade," she begged her sons. "It means life itself to me!"

Her eldest boy put on his straw sandals and set off eastward, in the direction the brocade had gone. After a month he came to a mountain cave. A stone horse stood outside, its mouth wide open as if it wanted to eat the red berries that grew on a tree nearby. An old woman appeared and he asked her if she had seen the brocade.

STEED OF STONE
Stone horses like the one in this story are a feature of ancient Chinese royal tombs. This one is at the tomb of Emperor Yang Ding Ging, in Gan Xian.

NATURE SPIRITS
Fairies in Chinese tales are female and beautiful – like the nymphs of Greek mythology. They have some magical powers, such as causing a wind to steal the widow's brocade in this tale. They may be mischievous, but are generally gentle and friendly. In stories, a lucky hero may win a fairy as a bride.

MYSTERIOUS PEAKS
This story is told by the Zhuang of the Guangxi region of southern China. The region has some spectacular "fairy-tale" scenery, such as the huge, teethlike rocks towering over rolling farmland in this picture.

"It has been stolen by the fairies of the Sun Mountain," came the reply. "To find them, you must pull out two of your teeth and put them in the stone horse's mouth. It will eat the red berries from yon tree and carry you over the Fire Mountain and the Sea of Ice to the Sun Mountain. But if you flinch while crossing the Fire Mountain, you'll be burned to a flake of ash; and if you shiver while crossing the Sea of Ice, you'll be frozen solid!"

The eldest son flinched and shivered even as she spoke, and the old woman said, "Don't go. This is too hard for you. Take this box of gold and spend it wisely."

He took the box of gold, but did not go home, because he didn't want to share it with his family.

Then the middle son set out, and the same thing happened to him as to his brother.

The horse carries the boy through the flames of the Fire Mountain

Finally, the youngest son set out, though he hated to leave his mother alone, lying in bed like a shriveled stick. When he reached the cave and the old woman offered him a box of gold, he said, "No. I must find my mother's wonderful brocade."

He knocked out two of his teeth and put them in the horse's mouth. The animal immediately came to life and ate the red berries. It carried the boy across the Fire Mountain. Though the fierce flames licked around him, he did not flinch. It carried him across the Sea of Ice. Though the bitter waves lashed him, he did not shiver. And so they came to the Sun Mountain, where he found the fairies in their hall, making a copy of the wonderful brocade. "You can have your mother's brocade back when we have finished," they said.

When darkness fell, the fairies hung from the ceiling a pearl that gave as much light as the sun. The prettiest fairy finished her work and stood back to compare their copy with the widow's work. She saw at once that the copy was not nearly as good and quickly stitched a little picture of herself onto the widow's brocade.

A moment later the youngest son picked up his mother's brocade and galloped away on the magic horse. They crossed the Sea of Ice and the Fire Mountain and soon found themselves back at the cave. The old woman took the teeth from the horse and put them back in the boy's mouth. The horse became cold stone once more.

The boy was soon home again. "Mother! I've got your brocade," he called. "Come outside and see!"

His mother was lying in bed as fragile as a splinter of tinder, but she dragged herself out into the sunshine. As she unfolded the brocade, a gentle breeze billowed under it. The wonderful brocade spread out, growing longer and wider until it covered the ground as far as the eye could see. The family's poor cottage vanished and they found themselves outside the big house from the picture, with its gardens and rich land. A beautiful girl was there with them.

"I am a fairy from the Sun Mountain," she explained. "I embroidered myself onto your brocade because I longed to live in this marvelous place."

So the widow and her youngest son settled down in the big house, and the son married the fairy.

One day two ragged beggars came to the edge of this magical land. They were the oldest brothers, who had wasted their gold in the city. When they saw the beautiful place that had grown from their mother's brocade, they were too ashamed to enter. They stumbled away, dragging their sticks in the dust.

The brocade becomes real and a fairy appears

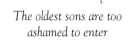

The oldest sons are too ashamed to enter

Easy Come, Easy Go

A shipwrecked old skipper catches a gull

HIGH-FLYING BIRD
The soaring seagull, a popular symbol of freedom, is a suitable helper for this story's free-spirited sailor.

WATERY LAND
Dikes are a feature of the Dutch countryside, helping drain the low-lying land or keep the sea at bay.

ONCE THERE WAS an old skipper who went to sea, but a whale came and broke his ship to pieces. The old skipper managed to keep afloat by clinging to the broken mast, and after a while the whale came back and threw him onto the beach. There the old skipper found a seagull that had lost its way. He caught the gull and shoved it underneath his jersey.

A farmer came riding along the dike and saw the old skipper shivering on the shore. "Go up to the farmhouse," the farmer shouted, "and my wife will give you something to eat and let you dry yourself by the fire."

When the old skipper reached the farmhouse, the farmer's wife was already entertaining the parson, so she wasn't pleased to have an old sailor dripping water all over the place. "You can dry off in the attic," she said. "But I've no food in the house."

However, when the old skipper peeped through a crack in the attic floorboards, he saw the farmer's wife bring out roast meat and three bottles of wine and set them on the table. He then heard her say to the parson, "Bread and water's good enough for my old man, but only the best will do for you."

Just then the farmer came home. His wife hid the meat in the pantry and the wine in the scullery, and the parson scrambled into a chest by the door. The farmer came in and asked, "Where's the old skipper?"

"Upstairs," his wife replied. "He wanted to be in the attic."

"Skipper, come down here!" called the farmer.

The skipper came downstairs with the gull still hidden beneath his jersey. He gave the gull a pinch and it cried out.

"What's that noise?" asked the farmer.

"It's a fortune-teller," said the old skipper. "It says there's roast meat in the pantry."

"Nonsense," said the farmer. "I haven't had roast meat for years." But when the farmer looked, he found a delicious roast.

The skipper gave the gull another pinch, and it cried out again. "What's it saying now?" asked the farmer.

"It says there are three bottles of wine in the scullery."

"Nonsense," said the farmer. "It's so long since I had any wine, I can't remember what it tastes like." But when the farmer looked, he found three bottles of the best wine money could buy.

"Wherever can that have come from?" his wife said nervously.

"The fortune-teller must have put it there," cried the farmer. "What will you take for it?" he asked the old skipper.

"A horse and wagon and that chest," the skipper replied.

The farmer helped the old skipper load the chest, in which the parson was still hiding, onto the wagon. The old skipper gave the farmer the gull and set off in the wagon. As he drove along the dike, he said aloud, "This chest is no use to me. I'll throw it in the sea."

Inside the chest, the parson groaned. "Now it's making horrible noises," said the old skipper. "I shall definitely throw it in the sea."

"Don't! Please don't!" the panic-stricken parson shrieked. "I'll fill this chest with money if you'll let me out!"

A LITTLE DRINK
The lure of the demon drink, by tradition the ruin of many a sailor, proves too much for the skipper, who celebrates in an inn similar to the one pictured here by David Teniers.

From the attic, the old skipper sees the farmer's wife hide the parson in a chest as her husband walks in

The farmer

The parson in the chest

The old skipper

The parson is so relieved to be let out of the chest that he fills it with money

The old skipper swaps his "fortune-telling" gull with the farmer for a horse and wagon and the chest

The old skipper opened the chest and let the parson out, and the parson filled the chest with money. "With all this money, I can buy myself a new boat," the skipper said to himself.

But on the way to buy the boat, he passed an inn. "I'll just have one drink to celebrate," he thought. One drink led to another and, after a week, the old skipper was down to his last penny.

"Ah, well," he sighed. "Easy come, easy go."

The old skipper fritters all the money away on beer

The Fisherman & His Wife

The fisherman and his wife live in a pigsty

One day the fisherman hooks a giant talking flounder

T HERE WAS ONCE a fisherman and his wife who lived in a pigsty by the sea. Every day the fisherman went fishing, and the wife stayed at home in the pigsty.

One day the fisherman was sitting with his rod, staring down into the clear water. Suddenly his line dipped down, down into the depths. When he hauled it in, he had caught a huge flounder. The flounder looked him in the eye and said, "Don't kill me. I am not a flounder, but an enchanted prince. Put me back in the water, please."

The cottage

First the flounder gives the fisherman and his wife a cottage to live in, then a castle

The castle

GOOD-LUCK CHARMS
Fish have ancient associations with good luck and were linked by the first Christians with Jesus, who miraculously fed five thousand people with "five loaves and two fish." The mosaic above is from a church built near the site of this miracle, near the Sea of Galilee, Israel.

The fisherman had never before heard a fish talk, and he willingly let it go free.

When he got back to the pigsty, he told his wife all about the talking flounder.

"What reward did you ask for?" she said.

"Why, nothing," he replied. "What could we want?"

"Somewhere better to live than this stinking pigsty for a start!" shouted his wife. "You go back this minute and ask that flounder to give us a cottage!"

The fisherman trudged down to the sea and called:
"Flounder, flounder, in the sea,
Come, come, come to me
For my wife, named Ilsabel,
Wants what I want not myself."

The flounder came swimming from the green and yellow waves and said, "What does she want?"

"She wants a cottage. She's fed up with living in a pigsty."

"Go home," said the flounder. "She has it already."

And sure enough, when the fisherman got home, there was his wife sitting on a bench outside the door of a neat little cottage.

For a fortnight the fisherman and his wife lived happily in their new home. But one morning the wife said, "This cottage is so poky. There's scarcely room to breathe. I think the least that flounder could have done, considering you set him free, was to give us a castle."

The fisherman was sent back to the sea to ask for a castle. The water was dark and foaming, but the flounder granted the wish.

When the fisherman got home, he found his wife standing on the steps of a great stone castle. Inside, the floors were paved with gleaming marble and the walls hung with rich tapestries. The furniture was of gold, and liveried servants were everywhere.

BIG FISH
This popular story, illustrated above by German artist Paul Hey, emphasizes that even the best luck can be pushed too far!

The next morning when they awoke and looked out of the window, the fisherman's wife said, "Look at all that country out there. There's no reason why we shouldn't be king of all that. Go and tell the flounder we want to be king."

So the fisherman went back to the sea. This time dark gray waves were breaking on the shore.

"What does she want now?" asked the flounder.

"She wants to be king," said the fisherman, shrugging his shoulders.

"So be it," said the flounder. "She is king already."

LAP OF LUXURY
This beautiful sitting room in Germany's Neuschwanstein Castle would have satisfied the fisherman's wife's wildest demands – at least for a little while.

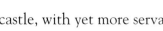

The fisherman's wife wants to be king – and her wish is granted

When the fisherman got home, his wife was living in an even grander castle, with yet more servants and guards to do her bidding. She was sitting on a high, golden, diamond-studded throne, with a golden crown on her head and a golden scepter in her hand.

"Now you are king," said the fisherman. "Let that be an end to it."

"Nonsense," snapped his wife. "For now I am king, I find time hanging heavy. I want to be emperor." So the fisherman went and asked the flounder to make her emperor. The sea was black and curdled, but the flounder granted the wish.

Soon, even being emperor wasn't grand enough. "I want to be pope," she cried. The fisherman went back to the sea, which was boiling and roaring. "Oh, dear," he said. "The flounder must be sick of granting wishes." But the flounder agreed to make his wife pope.

When he returned, he saw a cathedral surrounded by palaces. Inside was his wife, dressed in gold and sitting on a great throne. All the emperors and kings of the world were lining up to kiss her feet.

"You couldn't ask for anything more," said the fisherman.

"Perhaps not," she replied.

That night, the fisherman slept soundly, but his wife tossed and turned, wondering if there was something even more wonderful she could have asked the flounder for. She woke her husband up at sunrise and declared, "I want to be god."

"You're already pope!" he protested. But she screamed, tore her hair, kicked him, and chased him out of the palace. He ran down to the sea. A storm was raging and the sea seethed with huge black waves. The sky was a violent, angry red.

Shouting to be heard above the wind, the fisherman cried:
"Flounder, flounder in the sea,
Come, come, come to me,
For my wife, named Ilsabel,
Wants what I want not myself."

"What does she want now?" said the flounder.

"She wants to be god," stammered the fisherman.

"Go to her," said the fish. "You'll find her back in the pigsty." And they are living there still.

GONE TO POT
This story was contributed to the Grimms' collection by the painter Philipp Otto Runge. Similar tales are found in Scandinavia, Eastern Europe, France, England, and Italy, but the story is most popular in Germany and Russia. In some versions, the couple starts – and ends – living not in a pigsty (above), but in a potty!

The fisherman finds his wife back in the pigsty

The Poor Girl Who Became Queen

THERE WAS ONCE a poor cottager who lived with his daughter. She said he should go to the king and ask for a plot of land so they could grow enough food to live on. "If you will come with me, I will," he said.

So father and daughter set off for the king's palace. The king granted their request right away. Perhaps he was sorry for the poor cottager, or perhaps he liked the sparkle in the daughter's eye.

The cottager and his daughter lived happily on their little farm, till one day they dug up a golden mortar. The man said, "I should take this to the king."

His daughter replied, "Don't. He will only demand the pestle to go with it."

"Nonsense," he said. "The king will be mighty glad to have the mortar alone!"

How wrong can a person be? The king made a great fuss about the missing pestle, accused the man of stealing it, and threw him in prison. After two days, the jailer came to the king and begged him to let the cottager go. "He's making my life a misery wailing all day and all night 'If only I'd listened to my daughter! If only I'd listened to my daughter!'"

The puzzled king had the cottager brought before him, and the cottager explained how his daughter had warned him what would happen. "Go home," said the king, "and send your daughter to the palace."

When the king met the daughter again, he remembered the sparkle in her eye, and decided to test her to see if she was as clever as she seemed. So he said, "Come back here tomorrow neither clothed nor unclothed, and neither riding nor walking nor being carried."

The next day he waited for her, and soon he heard the distant braying of a donkey. When the donkey came into view, it was pulling a great bundle of fishing nets.

PEASANT QUEEN
Known in the fairy tales of the Brothers Grimm as "The Peasant's Wise Daughter," this retelling is based on a tale collected by Patrick Kennedy in County Wexford (above). More than 680 versions of this story have been collected in Ireland.

The wise girl advises her father not to take the golden mortar to the king

After passing the king's test, the poor girl becomes his queen

DONKEYS OF IRELAND
Donkeys have been specially bred in Ireland for centuries and were commonly used for carrying goods and hauling loads. This one is pulling a cart that dates back to the mid-19th century.

HUNG OUT TO DRY
The shallow waters around the Irish coast have traditionally been excellent fishing grounds. Nets like those shown drying in this 19th-century photograph would have been ideal for the girl of this story to dress up in.

Wrapped in the nets was the cottager's daughter, naked but perfectly decent, and neither walking nor riding nor being carried.

The bullocks' owner

The bullocks' owner refuses to return the man's foal, saying it is their child. The foolish king agrees

She was standing on the net and the donkey was dragging her along. "Brave girl!" laughed the king. "You're the bride for me!" And he married her, just like that.

One day two countrymen came to the palace. One had a horse, a mare, and a foal, and the other had two bullocks. The foal got in among the bullocks, and when its owner tried to get it back, the other man wouldn't let him. "This foal belongs to the bullocks," he said. "Why, you can see how fond they are of each other. It would break those bullocks' hearts to take their child away from them."

The man with the horse and mare complained to the king, but the king, who had never been a farmer, believed the man with the bullocks and let him keep the foal.

The man with the horse and mare remembered that the queen was a cottager's daughter, and he went to her with his problem…

The next day, while the king was out for his morning walk, he found the countryman on his hands and knees in the road, casting a net in the dust. "What are you doing?" he asked.

"Fishing," the man replied.

"You'll not catch any fish on the high road," laughed the king.

"I will, Your Majesty," said the man. "Or, at least, as many fish as you'll get foals from a pair of bullocks."

"Who put you up to this?" roared the king. The man confessed that the queen had told him what to do and say.

Now the king felt that the queen had shown him up to be a fool. He was so angry that he told her, "I can see you're more at home with peasants' quarrels than the duties of a queen, so back to your cottage you shall go. But, since you've been a good wife, I will let you take with you whatever you value most in the palace."

"All right," said she. "But let's have one last meal together."

When the king woke up after that meal he thought he was in a damp, dark prison cell. He called in alarm for his servants, but none came. He called louder still. In came the queen, his wife.

"Where am I?" he asked.

"Why, with me, in the cottage where I was born," she laughed. "You told me I could take whatever I valued most from the palace, so I gave you a sleeping draught and brought *you* along with me!"

Later, the king finds the man fishing by the roadside, and learns that the queen has made a fool of him

Then the king saw what a headstrong fool he had been.

"You are not just clever," he said, "but wise as well. Come home with me and be my queen again."

And back they walked to the palace, arm in arm.

POOR FAMILY'S HOME Parts of Ireland still contain tumbledown cottages similar to the one the king finds so dismal in this tale. Irish peasants lived hard lives scratching a livelihood from the soil. When crops failed – as in the Potato Famine of the 1840s – disaster and death often followed.

Banished to her bare cottage by the king, the girl turns the tables on him – by tricking him into coming with her!

KINGS OF THE CASTLE Rich Irish landowners had imposing homes, none more so than Kilkenny Castle. Occupied for centuries by the Butler family, it is one of the most spectacular castles in southeastern Ireland, and would have been a fitting home for the king in this story.

Heroes & Heroines

Courage and steadfastness are two of the most important qualities of a fairy-tale hero and heroine. They are the ones who do and dare. If a magic beanstalk sprouts outside their window, they unhesitatingly climb up it to see what is at the top. If they find themselves married to a murderer, or persecuted by a wicked stepmother, or threatened by a monstrous flying head, they keep their nerve and their wits about them. Though some people think fairy-tale heroines are weak and simpering dolls, this could not be farther from the truth. Many tellers of fairy tales were women, and the heroines of many stories are as resourceful and brave as any man – even if, as in "The Girl Who Pretended To Be a Boy," some have to wear boy's clothes to prove it.

Soliday bravely lures the monstrous Man-Crow down from its tree and lets fly with an arrow

❧ Little Red Riding Hood ☙

T HERE WAS ONCE A pretty little village girl. Everyone loved her, especially her grandmother, who had made her a red cloak with a hood that she wore so often people used to call her Little Red Riding Hood.

One morning her mother baked some bread and said to her, "Go and see how your poor old grandmother is, and take her a loaf and a pot of butter."

So Little Red Riding Hood set off to visit her grandmother, who lived in a village on the other side of forest. Walking through the woods, she met a wolf.

On the way through the woods to her grandmother's cottage, Little Red Riding Hood meets a wolf

He asked her where she was going and the poor girl, who did not know that it is dangerous to stop and chat with wolves, said, "I'm taking this loaf and pot of butter to my grandmother."

"Is it far?" asked the wolf.

"She lives in the first house in the village beyond the trees."

"I'd like to meet her, too," said the wolf. "You take the path on the left, I'll take the path on the right, and we'll see who gets there first."

With that, the wolf bounded off down the right-hand path, which led straight to the village. Little Red Riding Hood dawdled along the longer path, stopping to pick her grandmother a pretty little bunch of wayside flowers.

The wolf soon arrived at grandmother's house. He knocked – rat! tat! – on the door.

"Who's there?"

"It's your granddaughter, Little Red Riding Hood," said the wolf, in a high-pitched voice. "I've brought you a loaf and a little pot of butter that my mother has sent you."

The grandmother, who was in bed since she wasn't feeling well, called out, "Lift the latch and let yourself in."

The wolf went into the cottage, leaped upon the poor old woman, and gobbled her up. Then he closed the door and tucked himself up in bed to wait for Little Red Riding Hood.

Soon she came and knocked – rat! tat! – at the door.

"Who's there?"

When Little Red Riding Hood heard the wolf's hoarse voice, she was frightened, but then she remembered that her grandmother hadn't been well. Thinking that she must have caught a bad cold indeed, she replied, "It's your granddaughter, Little Red Riding Hood. I've brought you a loaf and a little pot of butter."

The wolf called out, "Lift the latch and let yourself in."

Little Red Riding Hood went into the cottage. The wolf, who was hiding under the bedclothes, shouted, "Put the loaf and butter in the bread bin and climb into bed with me."

So Little Red Riding Hood climbed into bed with the wolf.

"Grandmother! What big arms you have!" she said.

"All the better to hug you with, my dear," came the hoarse reply.

"Grandmother! What big legs you have!"

"All the better to chase you with, my dear!"

"Grandmother! What big ears you have!"

"All the better to hear you with, my dear!"

"Grandmother! What big eyes you have!"

"All the better to see you with, my dear!"

"Grandmother! What sharp teeth you have!"

"All the better to eat you with!"

And the wolf leaped upon Little Red Riding Hood and gobbled her up.

A TASTE OF GRANNY In earlier word-of-mouth tellings, the wolf tricks the heroine into eating some of her dead grandmother. In the end, she escapes by saying she has to go to the bathroom – outside the cottage! In other versions, the wolf is killed by a hunter. However in the 1984 movie A *Company of Wolves*, above, the wolves come out on top.

Little Red Riding Hood scrambles into bed with "Grandmother"

The Dancing Water

BAD SISTERS
This particular version
of this widespread tale
was collected in Sicily.
A similar story appears
in *The Arabian Nights*
under the title "Farizad
of the Rose's Smile."
Like other famous tales,
such as "Beauty and the
Beast" and "Cinderella,"
this story features two
older sisters ganging up
on the youngest.

THERE WERE ONCE three sisters who made their living by spinning thread. The king of their country used to go out after dark and listen at doors and windows to hear what his people were saying. One night he chanced to listen outside the very house where the sisters lived.

The oldest sister said, "If only I could marry the king's butler, I could drink as much as I wanted." The middle one said, "If only I could marry the king's valet, I could have as many clothes as I wanted." And the youngest said, "If only I could marry the king himself, I would bear him three children: two sons with apples in their hands, and a daughter with a star on her brow."

The next day the king summoned the girls and asked them to tell him honestly what they wished for. They did so, and he married the eldest to his butler and the middle one to his valet. Then he turned to the youngest and asked, "Will you marry me?" And she said yes.

Once she was queen, her sisters grew jealous. It no longer seemed enough to be married to the king's butler or the king's valet. They hid their hatred behind smiles.

The queen's babies are stolen by her jealous sisters, who put puppies in their places

While the king was away fighting a war, the queen gave birth to two boys with apples in their hands and a girl with a star on her brow. But the jealous sisters stole away her babies and put puppies in their places. When the king heard rumors that his wife had given birth to three puppies, he ordered her to be put on a treadmill as punishment.

The sisters abandoned the babes in the countryside, thinking they would be eaten by wild animals. But instead three fairies found them. "What beautiful children," said the first fairy. "I will give them a deer as a nurse."

"I will give them a purse that is always full of money no matter how much is taken out of it," said the second fairy.

"And I," said the third fairy, "will give them a ring that will change color when any misfortune befalls one of them."

The deer looked after the children until they were grown up. Then the first fairy came to visit and advised them to rent a house opposite the king's palace. They did so, and were soon recognized by their mother's jealous sisters, for the boys still had apples in their hands, and the girl a star on her brow.

Fearing that the children might be planning revenge on them, the two sisters pretended to be friendly. The eldest said to the girl, "You have such a lovely house. It's such a shame it lacks the three things that would make it perfect."

"What are they?" asked the girl.

"Why, the Dancing Water, the Singing Apple, and the Speaking Bird," the other sister replied. "But if your brothers really love you, they will get them for you."

The eldest brother set off in search of the Dancing Water. On his way he met three hermits – the three fairies in disguise. They told

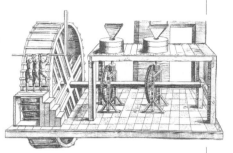

The Dancing Water   *A giant*

The Dancing Water is protected by four giants and four lions. All the while the eldest boy searches for it, his poor mother is walking the treadmill in prison

WILD CHILD
Legends and stories abound of children being raised by animals. The children in this tale are brought up by a deer; a wolf nursed Romans Romulus and Remus. But perhaps the most famous "wild child" of all is Mowgli (above, played by Sabu in a 1942 film), hero of Rudyard Kipling's *The Jungle Book*.

him, "Climb the mountain, and you will come to a palace with a gate guarded by four giants with swords in their hands. If the giants' eyes are closed, enter. If they are open, do not. Inside, you will find four lions, guarding the Dancing Water. If their eyes are open, bide your time. When they shut their eyes, you can take the water."

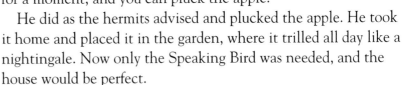

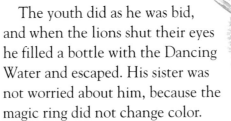

The Dancing Water dances from one golden basin to another

The youth did as he was bid, and when the lions shut their eyes he filled a bottle with the Dancing Water and escaped. His sister was not worried about him, because the magic ring did not change color.

When he came home, he put two golden basins in the garden and poured the Dancing Water into one of them. The water leaped constantly from one basin to the other in a beautiful arc, all the colors of the rainbow.

Next the second brother went in search of the Singing Apple. The hermits told him to climb to the palace. Inside he would find a tree on which the Singing Apple hung. "The tree sways back and forth, but if you bide your time, it will be still for a moment, and you can pluck the apple."

When the tree stops swaying, the second son plucks the Singing Apple

He did as the hermits advised and plucked the apple. He took it home and placed it in the garden, where it trilled all day like a nightingale. Now only the Speaking Bird was needed, and the house would be perfect.

The elder brother set out once more. The hermits said, "Climb the mountain and enter the palace. You will find a garden full of statues. In a basin in a fountain is the Speaking Bird. If it speaks to you, do not reply. Pick a feather from its wing, dip it into a jar you will find there, and anoint all the statues, and all will be well."

SICILIAN HILLS
This story evokes the distinctive landscape of Sicily with its many hills and mountains. In summer, the hot, dry *sirocco* wind dries up all rivers and streams, making the Dancing Water appear doubly miraculous and beautiful.

The brother climbed the mountain and found the bird. It said, "Your aunts have sent you to your death and your mother is imprisoned and on the treadmill."

"My mother on the treadmill?" exclaimed the boy, and instantly he turned into a stone statue.

At home, the sister saw her magic ring change color from blue to red. "Something has happened to our brother!" she said. So the younger brother set out; but the same thing happened to him. Waiting at home, the girl saw her magic ring turn from red to black.

She met the hermits, climbed the mountain, reached the palace with its garden full of strange statues, and found the Speaking Bird. It said, "Are you here, too? Then you will suffer the same fate as your brothers. Do you not see them? One, two, and you make three.

Your father is at the war. Your mother is imprisoned and on the treadmill. Your aunts are rejoicing."

But the brave girl did not reply. Instead she picked a feather from the bird's wing, dipped it in the jar, and anointed her brothers' statues. Instantly, they came to life again. They anointed all the other statues, and brought them all back to life. Then they returned home with the Speaking Bird.

The king had recently arrived home from the wars, and the brothers with apples in their hands and the sister with a star on her brow invited him to a banquet. When he saw them, he was amazed. He said, "If I did not know my wife had given birth to three puppies, I would think these were my children."

The king admired the ever-changing glories of the Dancing Water and the exquisite music of the Singing Apple. Then he said to the Speaking Bird, "Do you have nothing to say?"

YACKETY-YAK! The Speaking Bird could have been based on travelers' tales of the mynah bird of Asia (above). One of the bird world's finest mimics, this member of the starling family excels at imitating human speech.

Stone statues

With a touch of the Speaking Bird's feather, she brings her brothers back to life

The girl's ring changes color – something has happened to her brothers!

The Speaking Bird

The bird replied, "These are your sons, with apples in their hands. This is your daughter, with a star on her brow. The queen, your wife, is on the treadmill, reduced to skin and bone."

And so the king learned the truth. He rescued his wife from the treadmill, and loved her truly from that day on. But her sisters he ordered to be thrown into a cauldron of boiling oil.

The treadmill

The king rescues his wife from the treadmill

The Girl Who Pretended to be a Boy

EQUAL OPPORTUNITY
This Romanian story of a girl who dresses up as a fully armored knight to protect her father's kingdom is also told in Greek, Italian, Czech, and Russian versions.

ONCE UPON A TIME there was an emperor who conquered countries all over the world. Every time he conquered a new one he made its king send one of his sons to serve him for ten years as the price of peace.

The king of one country held out for many years, but at last he, too, had to submit. But how could he ask for peace? He had no son; only three daughters. They saw that he was unhappy and asked him the reason. "If only one of you were a boy!" he sighed.

"We may be girls, but we are not useless," they cried.

"Oh, yes," said the king, "you can spin, sew, and weave. But can you wield a sword and face down your enemy on the field of battle?"

"I can try," said the eldest, springing to her feet. "For am I not a princess and the daughter of a king?"

She dressed in man's clothes and mounted the most spirited horse in the stable, with eyes of flame and a coat of shining silver, and set out to prove her courage.

Unknown to his daughters, the old king was a magician. He hid beneath a bridge in the shape of a huge gray wolf, and when his daughter approached, he sprang out, baring his fangs and uttering a fearsome growl. The terrified girl turned tail and did not stop until she was back home in the palace.

The king used his magic to be there before her. When she dismounted, he hugged her and said, "Thank you for trying, my dear, but flies do not make honey."

Then the second daughter tried, but she could not face the wolf either. Then it was the youngest daughter's turn. The king said, "Do you think you are braver than your sisters, little one?"

The old king wishes he had a son to make peace with a warlike emperor

His youngest girl is determined to show she is as brave as any boy

"No," she replied, "but for your sake, father, I would cut the devil into pieces or become a devil myself. I will not fail."

The girl went into the stables, but instead of the silver stallion, she chose her father's ancient warhorse, Sunlight. Old and worn-out as he was, she knew she could trust him with her life.

When the wolf sprang at her, its claws like saws and its mouth as wide as an oven, she drew her sword, charged straight at it,

The girl defeats a wolf, a lion, and a many-headed dragon to prove her bravery, and the king sends her to the emperor as his son, Fet-Fruners

She dresses in armor and chooses her father's old warhorse, Sunlight

and the animal whined and slunk away. At the next bridge the king waylaid her in the shape of a fierce lion, but again she charged it down.

At the third bridge, the king met her in the shape of a dragon with twelve writhing heads breathing fire. She sliced off one of the heads with her sword and the dragon turned into her father. "Well done!" he said. "You are the best and bravest daughter, and wise, too, for you have chosen the right horse, who will give you good advice. Go to the emperor with my blessing. Tell him you are my son, Prince Fet-Fruners."

When she had ridden a few miles, she saw a curl of golden hair lying like sunshine on the road. "Should I pick this up, or let it lie?" she wondered.

Sunlight, the horse, spoke up, "If you pick it up, you will regret it. But if you let it lie, you will regret that, too. So take it."

The golden curl

BIBLICAL MONSTER
The dragon Fet-Fruners fights may have been inspired by the Hydra, destroyed by the Greek hero Heracles, or by the seven-headed serpent in the Book of Revelation in the Bible (above, a 15th-century illustration).

MAGNIFICENT EMPIRE
This story, with its mention of an all-conquering emperor, reflects the fact that from the 15th to the early 20th century most of what is now Romania belonged to the Ottoman Empire. The most famous emperor was Suleiman I (above), nicknamed the Magnificent. The empire was not popular and Romanian lords frequently rebelled.

UGLY MUG
As hideous as this 15th-century portrait, ogresses are gigantic women with a taste for human flesh. The one in this story has stilt-like legs for striding over the ocean and ape-like arms for swinging through the trees.

The princess hung the curl safely around her neck. Sunlight told her, "That golden curl belongs to the Princess Iliane, the most beautiful girl in the world."

The princess reached the court of the emperor, and told him her name was Prince Fet-Fruners. She was so cheerful and willing to undertake any task that she was soon the emperor's favorite among all his pageboys, each of whom was the son of a king.

One day the emperor noticed the golden curl and asked Fet-Fruners about it. She replied, "This curl belongs to Princess Iliane, the most beautiful girl in the world."

"I am the most powerful man," said the emperor, "so the most beautiful girl should be my wife. If you do not bring her to me, you shall lose your head."

Fet-Fruners asked Sunlight for advice. The horse replied, "Ask the king for a ship filled with treasure, and sail to the island where an ogress keeps Princess

Fet-Fruners The emperor

The emperor orders Fet-Fruners to bring him Princess Iliane, the most beautiful girl in the world, whom he wishes to have for a wife

Iliane captive. Pretend to be a merchant and ask the princess to come aboard to see your goods. Then you can steal her away."

Fet-Fruners did as Sunlight advised. As she sailed away with the princess, the ogress chased the ship. With each stride, one of the ogress's legs reached up to heaven while the other plunged through the waves to the bottom of the sea. When the ship reached land, the ogress was right behind.

Sunlight was waiting on the shore, and Fet-Fruners and the princess jumped on his back. Sunlight said, "Put your hand in my left ear, take out a stone, and throw it behind you."

Fet-Fruners did so and the stone became a mountain. But the ogress clambered over it with ease.

Sunlight told Fet-Fruners to take a brush from his left ear and throw it

An ogress pursues Fet-Fruners and Princess Iliane

behind. It became a forest, so tangled not even a wren could pass through it. But the ogress climbed a tree and swung from branch to branch like a hideous ape.

On the emperor's orders, Fet-Fruners steals a flask of holy water and is turned into a man by an angry hermit

At last Sunlight said, "Take the ring from Princess Iliane's finger and throw it behind you." The ring turned into a tower of stone. The ogress leaped to the top, fell down inside the ring, and broke into pieces at the bottom. Then Fet-Fruners put the ring back on the princess's finger.

The emperor was delighted when they arrived at court, but the princess said, "I have sworn to marry only the man who brings me the flask of holy water that is kept in a little church by the Jordan River and guarded by a hermit."

The emperor never did anything for himself; it was second nature to him to bark, "Fet-Fruners, go and fetch it!"

With Sunlight's help, Fet-Fruners managed to steal the water. As they made their escape, the enraged hermit called down a curse upon them: "If you are a man, may you become a woman; but if you are a woman, may you become a man!"

So Fet-Fruners turned into a real prince.

When they returned with the flask, the emperor said to the beautiful Princess Iliane, "Now will you marry me?"

"No," she replied, "for Fet-Fruners has brought me the holy water, not you."

The emperor was so angry he choked to death. Fet-Fruners gained his empire, married the princess, and they lived happily ever after.

When the princess wants to marry Fet-Fruners, the emperor chokes to death from rage

Man-Crow

JUNGLE LAIR
This story is set amid the lush, tropical jungle of Jamaica's hilly interior. It is here that the monstrous Man-Crow has his lair.

ONCE THERE WAS a giant bird in the woods named Man-Crow. When Man-Crow spread his wings, the world was cast into darkness. The king offered a great reward to anyone who could kill Man-Crow and make the world light again. He also promised that the victor could marry one of his daughters. Thousands of men went into the woods to kill Man-Crow. They found him, perched on one of the tallest trees, but they couldn't kill him.

One day a poor boy named Soliday said to his grandmother, "I am going to see if I can kill Man-Crow."

His grandmother answered, "Don't be stupid, boy!"

But Soliday went to Kingston to buy a bow and six arrows and then set out. When he found Man-Crow, he sang, "Good morning to you, Man-Crow, good morning to you, Man-Crow, good morning to you, Man-Crow, how are you this morning?"

And Man-Crow jumped down to the first branch and answered "Good morning to you, Soliday, good morning to you, Soliday, good morning to you, Soliday, how are you this morning?"

Anancy

Soliday

Soliday fires an arrow at Man-Crow

Soliday shot an arrow at Man-Crow and two of his feathers flew out. He sang his song again, and Man-Crow jumped down to the second branch and answered as before. Soliday shot a second arrow and two more of Man-Crow's feathers flew out. And so the singing and shooting went on. At every song Man-Crow moved down one branch, and Soliday fired an arrow.

Soliday sang the song for the sixth time and Man-Crow jumped down one more branch. Soliday shot his last arrow and Man-Crow fell to the ground, dead. Anancy saw it all from a tree.

*Anancy hides
in the rafters*

Soliday cut out Man-Crow's golden tongue and golden teeth, put them in his pocket, and went straight home to tell his grandmother.

Anancy came down from his tree, heaved Man-Crow's body over his shoulder, and walked across the bush to rap at the king's gate.

"Who's there?"

"It's me, Anancy. I've killed Man-Crow."

The gate was thrown open and the king welcomed Anancy into his house. Cunning Anancy immediately wed the prettiest of the king's daughters and everyone started feasting to celebrate the death of Man-Crow. Only Anancy couldn't really enjoy the feast, because he had one eye on the door in case Soliday should come.

Suddenly there was a knock at the gate. "Excuse me a moment," said Anancy, and, when everyone else went to see who was outside, he stole away from the table. Another knock rattled the gate's hinges.

"Who's there?" everyone shouted.

"It's me, Soliday. I've killed Man-Crow!"

"That's not possible. Anancy has killed Man-Crow."

Soliday showed them the golden tongue and teeth. The king looked in the mouth of dead Man-Crow, and saw that its tongue and its teeth had indeed been cut out. He then noticed that the door to his own house was shut fast. He shouted for Anancy.

*The king looks in Man-Crow's mouth and realizes
that Soliday has told the truth*

"Just coming!" Anancy called from within.

After a minute or two, the king shouted for him again.

"Won't be a moment!" called Anancy. "I don't feel well."

All this time, while the king waited angrily outside, Anancy was making a hole in the roof. He was so ashamed. At last the king lost patience and kicked down the door. Anancy was nowhere to be seen.

Some say he's still lost, up there in the rafters.

So the king married his prettiest daughter to Soliday instead, and made him one of the richest men in the world.

ANANCY

Anancy is a happy-go-lucky rogue who relies on cunning to fool the powerful. He is lazy and loves to claim praise when he has not earned it, as in this story. Stories of this trickster, who frequently takes the form of a spider, originally came from Ghana in West Africa, and were adopted and added to by the Afro-Caribbean peoples of the West Indies.

SEAPORT CAPITAL

This print of Kingston, the town where Soliday buys his bow and arrows, dates from the 19th century, when Jamaica was under British colonial rule. A thriving port since the 1690s and the capital of Jamaica since 1872, Kingston is situated on the southeastern coast of the island.

Kahukura & the Net Makers

SPECTACULAR COAST
With its many islands, fjords, and bays, the New Zealand coast is a perfect setting for this story of a young man's encounter with fairy fishermen.

IN THE OLD DAYS the people used to catch fish one at a time with hooks and lines. Sometimes they had to go hungry, because not enough fish were caught.

One time a clever young man named Kahukura was traveling up the coast. As he walked along the beach, he came to a spot where a huge catch had been landed. Nearly a thousand fish had been caught, but, to his amazement, there were only enough footprints for a few people. He realized that this enormous catch must belong to the patupaiarehe, the fairies. But how had they made it?

Kahukura hid near the beach, determined to find out the answer. Night came on and he heard voices out on the water, singing:

"Pull in the net! Work with a will!
The harvest of the sea writhes and twists
This way and that! Pull in the net!"

Kahukura had no idea what the song could mean – no one had ever used a net to catch fish before!

As he watched from the darkness, he saw moonlight glisten on

Kahukura is puzzled to see a large catch on the sand – surely only the fairy patupaiarehe could have caught so many fish

the pale bodies of a group of patupaiarehe. They began pulling on a rope dangling over the side of their canoe, singing their song once again, for the patupaiarehe were cheerful people, and they were in good spirits that night.

Now Kahukura was a fair-skinned man, like the patupaiarehe, and as they were hauling their

That night, he hears voices singing out on the water

net up the beach, he joined them at their work. In the darkness he looked like them, and they did not notice him. All night long he worked, till the patupaiarehe had once more caught upward of a thousand fish.

Toward dawn the patupaiarehe began to divide up their catch. "Hurry up," their leader called, "and finish before the sun comes up." For if the sun's rays ever touch the pale bodies of the patupaiarehe, they die.

Kahukura tried to string his share of the fish onto a length of flax like the others, but the knot kept giving way so that all the fish fell off. This happened so many times that he delayed the patupaiarehe until dawn. As the first light came into the sky, they saw that he was a man, and they fled, shivering and shouting, into the sea. They left all their fish behind, and their precious net. And Kahukura saw that their canoes were not canoes at all, but just sticks of flax.

SEA PEOPLE
The sea plays a prominent part in Maori folklore. The Maoris were originally a seafaring people – they first came to New Zealand in canoes from the islands of Polynesia. Fishing was essential to their livelihood, and they found plenty of fish, such as snapper and tarahiki, around the coast.

Eager to discover the fairies' fishing secret, Kahukura helps them haul in their catch

In the dawn light, he is spotted

The patupaiarehe flee, leaving their fish, and their precious net, behind

And this is how men learned to fish with a net, so that many fish can be caught, instead of just a few.

THE CHIEF'S STORY
This tale was narrated to Sir George Grey, a former governor of New Zealand, by the warrior-chief Te Wherowhero, pictured above in an 1844 painting. It was first published in Grey's *Polynesian Mythology* in 1855.

The Demon in the Jug

FALLEN ANGELS
The evil spirit of this
story resembles the
demons, or *jinn*, of
Arabic mythology and
the *Arabian Nights* tales.
Jinn are fallen angels
that can assume animal
or human shape. Some
are beautiful and good,
others hideous and evil.
The frightening one
above was painted by
René Bull.

ONCE UPON A TIME a man became lost while walking through a forest. He sat down on a hollow log to rest and, reaching inside it, found a sealed jug. Thinking it might contain something to drink, he pulled out the cork. Instead of liquid, a cloud of smoke poured out. It billowed into the air and shaped itself into a huge spirit, roaring with laughter.

The man was very afraid, but also hopeful, for he had heard stories of men who had been well rewarded for freeing such spirits.

The spirit spoke, as if reading the man's thoughts. "I owe you thanks for releasing me from that jug, in which I was imprisoned long ago by my enemy. In return, I will grant you three wishes."

Overjoyed, the man cried, "My first wish is to go home, for I have been wandering, lost in this forest."

A man finds a jug, pulls the cork, and smoke pours out …

He forgot to ask who the enemy was who had imprisoned the spirit. If he had, he would have learned that it was that holy man the Baal Shem Tov who, when only a boy, had faced down this *jinni* – in truth, a wicked demon – sealed it in a jug, and hidden the jug deep in the forest.

All the man could think of was what to ask for as his final two wishes. Should it be riches, or power, or both? When they reached his home, the spirit said to him, "I advise you to sleep on the matter. You do not want to waste your wishes!" And the man agreed.

When he awoke next morning, however, he found he could barely move! His bed was only half its normal size – and the same was true of everything else in the house. Even the money in his purse was only half what it had been. He went into the kitchen and there, sitting at the half-size table like some hulking great lad, was the demon.

"Make everything in my house its proper size and never meddle with it again!" the man shouted.

"Your wishes are my commands," cackled the demon. It waved its hand, and everything went back to normal.

"What do you mean, wishes?" the man exclaimed.

"Why, you asked me to make everything its proper size, and I have done so," said the demon. "You also asked me never to meddle with it again and I will not. Those were your two remaining wishes. And as you have had three wishes, it's only fair I should have one. I wish that this house should be mine from now on!"

The smoke shapes itself into a demon, who grants the man three wishes

The man knew then what sort of a creature it was he had set free. He went to the Baal Shem Tov and begged him to help.

But the demon cheats, shrinking everything in the man's house

The Baal Shem Tov gave him holy amulets to hang in every room of the house. When the man hung up the last one, a kind of whirlwind swept out of the window; it was the demon, who could not bear to stay in a holy place.

With the help of a holy man, the Baal Shem Tov, the man drives the demon from the house

The next day, the Baal Shem Tov came himself to make sure the demon was gone. He searched everywhere, even in the cracks in the walls. Then he saw that the lid of the water barrel was ajar. He lifted it, and at once the whirlwind rose from the barrel.

Holy amulet

The Baal Shem Tov said, "Take your own shape, you creature of the dark!" And the whirlwind shaped itself, not into a laughing spirit, but a snarling demon. Then the Baal Shem Tov said, "Once before I confined you to a jug. Now I do so again. Begone, and never trouble this world again!"

The Baal Shem Tov walked toward the demon. Step by step, as he drew nearer, it grew smaller and smaller, until it was just a tiny, wailing figure, beating its wings against the sides of the jug. This the Baal Shem Tov quickly sealed.

The snarling demon is no match for the holy powers of the Baal Shem Tov, who imprisons it in a jug once more

103

Baba Yaga

THE WORST WITCH
Baba Yaga, shown here in a 1900 Russian illustration, is the best-known witch in Russian folklore. A hideous hag, sometimes described as having tusks, she preys on children and flies using a magic pestle and mortar instead of a broomstick. Luckily for the heroine of this tale, Baba Yaga, like most witches, is unable to cross running water.

PRETTY SCARVES
Peasant life may have been hard, but Russian women still found time to create beautiful embroidered kerchiefs like the one mentioned in this story. They were mostly worn on festive occasions, as depicted above in a 1902 painting by Andrej Rjabuschkin.

ONCE UPON A TIME a widower remarried and his new wife hated his daughter. She did everything she could to make her life a misery. One day when the father was away, the stepmother said, "Go to your aunt, my sister, and ask her for some sewing thread." Now the stepmother's sister was Baba Yaga Bonylegs, the witch who lives in the forest in a hut that stands on chicken's legs, so the girl suspected that her stepmother meant trouble.

When she got to Baba Yaga's hut, she asked to borrow some thread. Baba Yaga said, "Of course. But while I'm looking for it, sit and do some weaving." Once the girl was sitting at the loom, Baba Yaga called her maid and said, "Run my niece a bath, and make it good and hot. I want to eat her for breakfast."

The girl overheard this, begged the maid not to make the water too hot, and gave her a pretty kerchief as a reward. Then the girl heard Baba Yaga say to the cat, "You can scratch

The girl's stepmother sends her to visit the witch Baba Yaga, whose hut stands on chicken's legs

out my niece's eyes." But the girl gave the cat a piece of ham, and in return the cat gave her a comb and a towel. "Run," said the cat. "If you hear Baba Yaga on your tail, throw these behind you."

The girl ran out of the house. Baba Yaga's dogs leaped up at her as if to tear her to pieces, but she threw them some bread and they left her alone. Baba Yaga's gate tried to bang shut on her, but she oiled its hinges and it let her through. The birch tree outside the gate tried to lash her eyes, but she tied it back with a ribbon and it let her pass.

Meanwhile, the cat sat at the loom and wove instead of her, and whenever Baba Yaga called, "Are you weaving, dear?" the cat would reply, "I am weaving, Aunt." Soon, however, Baba Yaga came to see what was going on, and when she saw the terrible tangle the cat had made of the weaving, she flew into a rage. She beat the cat, but the cat said, "In all the years I have served you, you have never given me so much as a fish bone, but your niece gave me a piece of ham."

Baba Yaga's maid, cat, and dogs look on as their cruel mistress pursues the girl

Baba Yaga in her magic mortar

Racing across the sky, the witch seems sure to catch the girl – but the cat's magic gifts protect her

Baba Yaga beat her maid, and her dogs, and her gate, and her birch tree, but they all told her that her niece had treated them better than she ever had. So Baba Yaga mounted her magic mortar, and using her pestle to whip it on, set off in pursuit of her niece.

When the girl heard Baba Yaga close behind, she threw the towel behind her, and it turned into a wide, wide river. Baba Yaga gnashed her teeth with rage, for she could not cross running water. She flew back home and fetched her oxen. The oxen drank the river dry and then she could cross.

The girl heard Baba Yaga close behind her once more. She threw down the comb and it became a great, dark forest. Howling with fury, Baba Yaga began to gnaw through the trees, her sharp and twisty teeth cutting through trunks and branches. But just as the witch struggled out of the forest, the girl reached the door of her own house and slammed it shut behind her.

After that her father sent the wicked stepmother away, and he and his daughter lived together in happiness and prosperity.

The towel changes into a wide, wide river – but Baba Yaga's oxen drink it dry

The girl's house

The comb turns into a forest

Can the girl get home before Baba Yaga, with her twisty teeth, gnaws through the trees?

❧ The Flying Head ☙

BEYOND THE TREES
This tale was first recorded in 1902. It is told by the Iroquois peoples of northeastern North America, a region of rivers, lakes, and dense woods (above). Many Native American nations have stories of monsters that once preyed on humans.

POWERFUL MEDICINE
The power of the spirit world is reflected in this Iroquois mask, but here the power is for good, not evil. Carved from a basswood tree, this mask once belonged to a member of the False Faces, a group of healers. Each spring and summer the False Faces would visit longhouses exorcising evil spirits and curing ailments.

I N THE PAST, human beings were at the mercy of many terrible monsters and spirits. By day, the strong sun kept them at bay, but at night, and in storms, these spirits came out from their lairs to prowl the earth. The most terrible of all was the Flying Head. It was just a huge head without a body, four times as tall as the tallest man, with wings sprouting from its cheeks. It would fly up into the sky and then swoop down and seize some unlucky person in its terrible fangs. Its hair was filthy and matted, and its mouth was set in a snarl of rage.

One night a young Iroquois woman was sitting alone with her baby in the longhouse. Everyone else had fled for fear of the Flying Head, but the young woman had said, "We cannot let our children live in fear of this monster. Someone must make a stand."

She waited until the Flying Head appeared at the longhouse door. Then she pretended to be busy cooking a meal, picking up red-hot rocks with a forked stick and bringing them up to her face. The Flying Head couldn't see that she was dropping the rocks behind her, not eating them. She kept smacking her lips, exclaiming, "No one has ever tasted meat like this!"

The Flying Head gulps down red-hot rocks and screams in agony

The Flying Head rushed in and gulped down the rest of the fiery rocks. The rocks burned its throat, and it flew away, screaming, across the land. It screamed so loud the earth trembled, and the leaves fell from the trees. When the last screams had died away, the people took their hands from their ears and went back to the longhouse, where they found the brave young woman calmly feeding her baby. The terrible Flying Head was never seen again.

Jack & the Beanstalk

A POOR WIDOW HAD an only son, named Jack. Every morning she milked their cow, Milky-White, and Jack took the milk to market. But one morning Milky-White was dry and not one drop of milk fell into the pail.

"I'll get work," said Jack.

"Nobody would take a lazybones like you," his mother said. "There's only one thing for it. We must sell Milky-White."

So Jack set off for town with the cow. He hadn't gone far when he met a funny-looking man. "Good morning, Jack. And where are you off to?" asked the man.

"I'm going to market to sell our cow," replied Jack, wondering how the man knew his name.

"And you've the look of a proper businessman about you," the man smiled. "I bet you know how many beans make five."

"Two in each hand and one in the mouth," said Jack.

"I knew we could do business," the man said. "Because here they are, the very beans." The funny-looking man held out some funny-looking beans. "I'll let you have these beans for that cow."

"Milky-White's worth more than five beans!"

"Just as you like," said the man. "If you don't want my magic beans, I dare say others will."

"I didn't know they were *magic* beans!" Jack exclaimed. He took the beans and placed Milky-White's halter into the man's hand…

"Back already, Jack?" cried his mother. "And you've sold Milky-White! Good lad! How much did you get?"

"You'll never guess," said Jack. "I've done better than we ever thought!"

FULL OF BEANS
This woodcut is from the earliest-known printed version of the story, dating from 1730, in which Jack has several fantastic adventures at the top of the beanstalk.

A man offers Jack a handful of magic beans for Milky-White the cow

Bean
sprouting

"Oh, oh!" Jack's old mother gasped. "Let me sit down. Is it fifty pounds?"

The magic begins when Jack's mother spits one of the beans out the window

"No," grinned Jack.

"A hundred?"

"No," Jack laughed.

"Surely not a thousand?!"

"Better than that, Mother. I got five magic beans!" Jack held out his hand. The beans jiggled on his palm.

"Dolt! Nincompoop! Brainless ninny! A cow for a handful of beans! Off to bed! Not a sip shall you drink, not a bite shall you eat!" Poor Jack went hungry to bed. His mother tossed four beans on the fire. The last one she popped in her mouth and spat out the window.

When Jack awoke the next morning, the room was filled with a strange green light. Outside, a beanstalk reached up into the arching blue as far as he could see. Jack swarmed up this living ladder till he reached the sky. There he found a broad road leading to an enormous house. Standing on the doorstep was an enormous woman.

"Morning," said Jack. "Could you spare me a bite of breakfast?"

At the top of the beanstalk is an enormous house

"Breakfast?" the woman cried. " You'll be breakfast if you're not careful. My man's a giant, and partial to broiled boy!" But the giant's wife had a kind heart, so she took Jack into the kitchen and gave him bread and cheese and a jug of milk. Before Jack could finish his meal, thump! thump! thump! the house began to shake. "Quick!" she hissed. And she bundled Jack into the oven just as the giant came in.

He was a big one to be sure. He pulled three calves from his belt and threw them on the table. "Broil these for breakfast," he grunted. "Since we don't have any boy." His nose twitched and he bellowed: "Fee fie fo fum, I smell the blood of an earthly man. Be he alive or be he dead, I'll grind his bones to make my bread."

SOWING IN THE RAIN
Jack's magic bean might have been a runner type, the fastest growing and tallest bean. The story does not say what the weather was like when Jack's bean sprouted, but it is likely to have been wet if an English proverb is to be believed: "Sow beans in the mud, and they'll come up like trees."

SPITTING
The fact that Jack's mother spits the magic bean out the window may be significant. For, despite being frowned on in polite circles, spitting is supposed to bring good luck. This superstition is found all over the world.

The giant's wife

"Nonsense, dear," said his wife, "you're dreaming. Or perhaps you smell the scraps of that little boy you had yesterday."

After the giant had breakfasted he went to a chest and took out two bags of gold. Then he sat and slowly counted his gold pieces. After a while his head began to nod and his gigantic snores were soon rattling the kitchen pots and pans.

The giant counts out his money

Jack tiptoed from the oven, seized a bag of gold, and tucked it under his arm. He ran out of the house, reached the beanstalk, and climbed down. His mother was waiting anxiously at the bottom. "I told you they were magic beans," Jack laughed.

Jack escapes with a sack of gold

Jack and his mother lived in fine style thanks to the giant's gold, but at last every piece was spent, so Jack decided to climb the beanstalk again. When he reached the sky, he found the road and the house and the giant's wife, just as before.

"'Morning," said Jack, bold as brass. "What's for breakfast?"

"You're the youngster who was here before," frowned the giant's wife. "My man missed a bag of gold that day."

"Did he?" said Jack. "I dare say I could tell you something about that, but I'm so hungry I can't speak."

The gold spent, Jack tells his mother that he will climb up the beanstalk again

The giant's wife took him in and gave him some food, then thump! thump! thump! came the giant's footsteps. Jack hid in the oven once more.

TALL TALES
The idea of a stairway connecting heaven and earth, like the beanstalk in this story, is an ancient one, appearing in the Old Testament stories of the Tower of Babel and Jacob's Ladder. It is central to Norse myth, in which the underworld, the earth, and the heavens are connected by an ash tree, Yggdrasil.

———— ❧ ————

RIGHTEOUS ROBBER
A version of the story that appeared in an early magazine published by Benjamin Tabart in 1807 gives Jack a reason for stealing from the giant. A fairy informs Jack that, long ago, the giant murdered his father, and he should get revenge. She adds that Jack may take anything that the giant possesses, "for everything he has is yours, though now you are unjustly deprived of it."

A GOLDEN HEN
While, of course, no one has ever owned a hen that lays gold eggs, a good egg-laying hen was much prized in bygone times. Special breeding for egg-laying did not begun until the 19th century.

GOLDEN DONKEY
The giant's hen that lays golden eggs is echoed in other tales, including one collected by the Brothers Grimm in which the young hero acquires a magical donkey. At the command "Bricklebrit," it spits out gold pieces.

"Fee fie fo fum!" the giant roared. "Wife, bring me my hen that lays the golden eggs." When she had brought it, he said to the hen, "Lay!" and it laid an egg of solid gold. After a while the giant fell into a doze and began to snore. Jack crept out of the oven and tucked the hen under his arm. He raced to the beanstalk, with the hen clucking loudly: "Cack cack-a-dack, cack cack-a-dack!"

The giant stirred and mumbled, "Wife, what are you doing with my hen?" But Jack was already slithering down the beanstalk. He showed his mother the hen. "Lay!" he said, and the hen laid another gold egg.

Still Jack was not content. Though his mother begged him not to go, once again he swarmed up the beanstalk. This time he hid until the giant's wife came out of the house to hang up her washing. Then he sneaked in and hid in the empty washtub. Before long, thump! thump! thump! in came the giant, followed closely by his wife.

"Fee fie fo fum, I smell the blood of an earthly man," roared the giant. "I smell him, wife, I smell him."

"Do you, dear?" said his wife. "Well, if it's that rogue who stole your

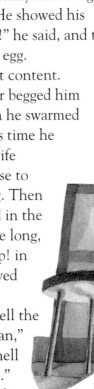

The giant's hen lays an egg of solid gold

Jack makes off with the magic hen

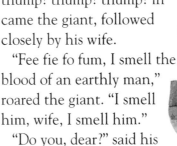

While the giant's wife hangs out the washing, Jack hides in the washtub

gold and your hen, he's sure to be in the oven." But Jack wasn't in the oven, and the giant's wife said, "There you are again, with your fee fie fo fum. You must be smelling the boy you caught last night, the one I've just broiled for your breakfast!"

The giant sat down at the table, but every now and then he muttered, "Well, I could have sworn..." and got up and searched the kitchen. Jack's heart fluttered like the washing in the wind, but the giant didn't think of looking in the washtub.

After breakfast he called, "Wife, bring me my golden harp!" She placed it on the table before him. "Sing!" he said, and the harp poured forth a stream of golden notes.

Soon the giant's head began to nod, and the harp's beautiful music was drowned by his thunderous snores.

Jack crept out of the washtub, grabbed the harp, and ran. But the harp cried out,

The giant

"Master! Master!" and the giant woke up. He spotted Jack scrambling down the beanstalk clutching the harp.

When Jack grabs the golden harp it cries out, "Master! Master!"

The giant jumped onto the beanstalk after Jack. The beanstalk shook with the giant's weight. As Jack reached the bottom he shouted, "Mother, help me!" His mother ran to the woodshed for the ax. Jack took it from her and hacked at the beanstalk until it toppled over. And as it fell, it flung the giant far away. He tumbled into the sea and drowned.

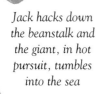

Jack hacks down the beanstalk and the giant, in hot pursuit, tumbles into the sea

Jack and his mother now had the hen to lay them golden eggs and the harp to sing them golden songs; and if they've not lost them, they have them still.

THE HARP
The harp is one of the oldest stringed instruments, dating back over 4,000 years. The giant's magic harp plays itself, but, ordinarily, harps are played with the thumb and fingers of both hands. Early harps were small enough to fit under Jack's arm. It is hard to imagine him escaping down the beanstalk with a heavy, 5.5 ft-high (170 cm) modern version!

GIANT KILLER
The theme of a huge, powerful character being outwitted and defeated by a far weaker one is central to many stories, including "Jack and the Beanstalk." This 17th-century painting by Orazio Borgianni shows David killing giant Goliath.

A Magic Whistle

WANDERING STARS
This tale is set in the outback of New South Wales, Australia, once famous for its swagmen, trappers, bushmen, and bushrangers.

ONCE IN THE AUSTRALIAN BUSH there was a young swagman named Damper. He was called that because he always said that damper bread, cooked in the ashes of an open fire under the stars, was the best food in the world.

One night as he lay on his back letting his supper go down, the darkness was suddenly lit up by a host of glow-worms and fireflies and Damper saw a troop of little figures, some dressed in black, some in gold, and some in white. He gave himself a punch or two on the head, muttering, "I'm not seeing straight." But when he looked again, the figures were still there.

Soon the tiny people began to dance, so fast it set Damper's senses reeling. But he noticed that two of them, the grandest of all, had fallen out of the dance. He decided that they must be the king and queen of this fairy host, so he tried to hear what they were saying.

He finds the whistle under a tree

The fairy king said, "I've hidden the magic whistle where no one can find it, under the roots of that old eucalyptus tree."

"Good," replied the queen. "For whoever found that whistle would be able to control any animal, bird, or man. For when it is played, any creature listening to it just has to dance."

In the morning Damper wondered if it had all been a dream. He decided to check under the roots of the old eucalyptus tree. There, sure enough, was a reed whistle, about six inches long, with a mouthpiece of pure gold.

Damper hears fairies talk of a magic whistle that can make every creature dance

Damper put the whistle in his bluey and went along the road. Soon he saw a cart coming in the other direction. A fat, angry woman was swaying on the cart, scolding a little man walking beside the horse.

Damper went up to the woman and asked her for a little food.

"Be off with you, you loafing rascal," she said.

Damper took out the whistle and began to play a lively jig. The fat woman threw herself from the cart and began to leap and cavort in the road, while the little man laughed fit to burst. After a bit Damper put down the whistle and she flopped down in the dust. When he raised the whistle to his lips again she begged him, "Stop, for mercy's sake! Take all the tucker in the cart."

Damper helped himself to a little of their tucker and went on his way, singing "Waltzing Matilda" at the top of his voice. But he swallowed his song when a big, bearded bushranger loomed up from nowhere, yelling, "Halt, or I'll fire."

Damper pulled out his whistle and began to play. The bushranger's horse started to galumph about the road with the bushranger hanging on for dear life. "Please, no more!" the bushranger begged. " I'll fill your pouch with gold."

"Not a bit of it," said Damper. "You'll hand over all of your ill-gotten treasure, and your horse as well, or you shall dance again!"

WILD COLONIAL BOYS Bushrangers were armed robbers who preyed on travelers. The most notorious was Ned Kelly, above, who terrorized northeastern Victoria with his gang in the 1870s. Other legends include Frank Gardiner, "King of the Bushrangers," Fred Ward, "The Thunderbolt," and "Gentleman" Matthew Brady.

When Damper plays the magic whistle, he makes a mean woman dance till she drops and persuades a bushranger to give up all his ill-gotten gains…

The bushranger began to curse, so Damper blew a single note on the whistle. "Stop! I agree," the bushranger cried. He handed over his revolver, his money belt, his boots, and his horse, and ran off. Damper looked in the belt. It was filled with gold. As he mounted the horse, he was the happiest boy in all Australia – and one of the richest, too.

… even his horse! The bushranger runs off into the bush, leaving Damper whooping with joy

Bluebeard

LA
BARBE BLEÜE.

L estoit une fois
un homme qui
avoit de belles
maisons à la Vil-
le & à la Campagne, de la
vaisselle d'or & d'argent, des
meubles en broderie; & des
ca-

NO TIME TO LOSE!
This first page of a
17th-century retelling
of "Bluebeard" by
Charles Perrault shows
Bluebeard about to kill
his wife. Meanwhile
her brothers rattle
across the castle
drawbridge to the
rescue. Will they be
in time?

THERE WAS ONCE a rich man named Bluebeard who possessed grand houses in the town and country, and everything his heart could desire, but no wife. A noble lady living nearby had two daughters, and Bluebeard asked her if one of them would consent to marry him. Neither of the girls wanted to marry a man with a blue beard, especially when they heard rumors that he had been married several times before, and no one knew what had become of any of his wives.

Nevertheless the girls agreed to go to his house in the country for a party that was to last a whole week, with nothing to do but hunt, fish, dance, picnic, and play games. It was all very much fun and, by the end of the week, the younger daughter had stopped worrying about the color of her host's beard. As soon as they got back to town, she and Bluebeard were married.

*Bluebeard throws a week-long party
at his splendid country house*

Bluebeard's future bride

*Bluebeard is very
attracted by the young
ladies and decides to
make one of them his wife*

After a month,
Bluebeard told his wife that he
had to go away on business.

*The guests picnic, play games, and hunt –
and one young girl falls in love*

"But there's no need for you to get bored," he said. "Ask your sister Anne to come and stay with you and enjoy the country air."

He gave her a large bunch of keys and told her what they were all for. This one would open the strongbox and that one the safe. There was just one tiny key that she must not use. That was for the door to a little room at the end of the great gallery, and he forbade her to open it. "If you do, you will rouse my anger."

She promised to do as she was told, and he went on his way.

Despite having her sister Anne to stay and all the marvelous things in Bluebeard's house, the young wife could not enjoy herself for she was eaten up by curiosity about what lay behind the door of the little room. She could think of nothing else. One afternoon, while Anne was busy at the other end of the house, she took the tiny key, opened the door, and entered the forbidden chamber.

FATAL CURIOSITY
In fairy tale, curiosity is often a female trait – and it almost always has dire consequences! Bluebeard, here illustrated by Gustav Doré, tells his new wife about the key as a cruel test of her obedience. Little does she know that the penalty for failure is death. As Charles Perrault wrote in 1697: "Curiosity… often brings with it serious regrets."

———— 🗝 ————

REAL BLUEBEARDS
Various historical figures have been cited as models for Bluebeard. These include 15th-century French nobleman and murderer Gilles de Rais, whose victims numbered 140, and the English king Henry VIII, responsible for the deaths of two of his six wives. Another candidate is Comorre the Cursed, who, in 6th- century Brittany, killed four wives when they became pregnant. His fifth wife, Tryphine, escaped and told all.

Before he leaves, Bluebeard warns his new wife never to use the tiny key…

…but she cannot resist a look in the forbidden chamber

As her eyes grew used to the gloom, she realized that the floor was sticky with clotted blood. She peered closer, then drew back in horror. Reflected in this crimson pool were the corpses of several women, hanging up along the walls of the forbidden chamber. These were Bluebeard's wives, whose throats he had cut, one after the other.

KEY CHANGE
In love stories, tiny keys have romantic associations, as the expression "key to my heart" testifies. This tale, however, cleverly turns this idea on its head, making a little key a frightening symbol of guilt.

The bloodstained key

Bluebeard sees blood on the key and realizes his wife has discovered his terrible secret

BAD NAME
Such was the fame of "Bluebeard" throughout Europe that mothers used to frighten their children by saying that Bluebeard would get them if they didn't behave. Even today, the media often call any man accused of killing his wife or lover a "Bluebeard."

She thought that she would die from fear. The key of the room fell from her hand onto the floor. Trembling, she picked it up and, locking the door behind her, went back to her bedroom, where she fell down in a faint.

When she awoke, she noticed that the key was stained with blood. She scrubbed and scrubbed, but the blood would not come off.

That evening, Bluebeard returned unexpectedly early from his travels and in the morning he asked her for his bunch of keys. When she brought them to him, he immediately noticed that one key was missing. A single glance at her pale face and trembling hand told him what had happened.

"Where is the key to the little room?" he asked.

"I must have left it upstairs," she replied.

"Bring it to me," he ordered.

Reluctantly, she fetched him the tiny key. As he took it, he glowered at her from behind his blue beard. "Why is there blood on this key?" he thundered.

"I'm sure I don't know," she whispered.

"Well, I do," he raged. "You couldn't resist going into that room when I told you not to. Well, since you wanted to go in there, you shall. You shall hang alongside the others!"

She flung herself at her husband's feet, begging for mercy. She might have wrung pity from a stone; but Bluebeard's heart was harder than any stone.

"You must die," he declared grimly. "Your last hour has come."

"At least give me a quarter of an hour," she pleaded, "so that I can say my prayers."

"If you must," frowned Bluebeard.

When she was back in her room, she called for her sister Anne and told her what had happened. "Sister, I beg you, go to the top of the tower and tell me if you can see our brothers coming. They promised to come and see us today." So Anne climbed to the top of the tower.

The wife called, "Anne, sister Anne, do you see anything coming?"

And Anne replied, "Nothing but the dust made gold by the sun and the green of the grass." Bluebeard set foot on the first stair, his huge cutlass in his hand.

"Anne, sister Anne, do you see anything coming?"

"Nothing but the dust shining gold in the sun, and the green grass growing." Bluebeard set foot on the second stair.

"Anne, sister Anne, do you see anything coming?"

"I see a cloud of dust in the distance," Anne replied.

"Is it our brothers?"

"No, sister, only a flock of sheep." Bluebeard set foot on the third stair.

"Anne, sister Anne, do you see anything coming?"

"I see two riders approaching," she replied. "God be praised! It is our brothers. Oh, hurry! Hurry!"

Bluebeard entered the room.

His wife once more begged for mercy. "Be quiet," he said. "You must die." He seized her by the hair, his cutlass at her bare throat.

At that moment her two brothers burst in, swords in their hands, and ran Bluebeard through the heart. Their poor sister lay on the floor, sobbing with terror and relief.

Bluebeard left no heirs, so his wife inherited all his wealth. She gave some money to Anne, so that she could marry her true love, and some to her brothers, so that they could become officers in the army. The rest she shared with her second husband, a good man, who helped her forget the terrible time she had spent with Bluebeard.

Sister Anne

The terrified wife calls out to her sister as Bluebeard approaches

Bluebeard climbs the stairs

STAIRWAY TO FEAR
This story is full of the classic ingredients of the horror story: a charming, but evil, villain, a terrible secret, and an innocent young heroine. The ending also features a superb suspenseful scene as the villain slowly climbs a flight of stairs toward his cowering victim. This situation has since featured in any number of spine-tingling tales and movies.

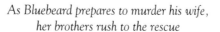

As Bluebeard prepares to murder his wife, her brothers rush to the rescue

The brothers

117

The Twin Brothers

A WOMAN ONCE gave birth to twin boys named Mavungu and Luemba. They were almost full-grown, and each boy brought his own luck into the world with him. About this time, the daughter of Chief Nzambi was ready to be married. The leopard, the gazelle, the pig, and every other animal offered themselves in turn, but Nzambi's daughter refused them all.

MAGIC FIGURE
Mavungu's "luck" might well have been similar to this 19th-century wooden figure, or fetish, from Zaïre. It would have been invested with power by a witchdoctor to protect its owner, bring wealth, and defend against enemies. Unfortunately, Mavungu's "luck" runs out in this story!

Mavungu

Chief Nzambi

Nzambi's daughter

The witch

Nzambi's daughter refuses all the animals and wishes to marry Mavungu

Mavungu sees a village in a mirror, travels there, and is killed by an old witch

VILLAGE LIFE
Though most Zaïrians now live in cities, in the country there are still many villages of small, thatched, dried-mud houses similar to the setting of this tale.

When Mavungu heard of this girl, he determined to marry her. He asked his luck for help and, after many days traveling, arrived at Nzambi's village. As soon as Nzambi's daughter caught sight of him, she ran to her mother and said, "I have seen the man I love, and I shall die if I do not marry him."

So they were married, and after the wedding they were led to a fine hut, while all the village danced and sang for gladness.

In the morning Mavungu saw that the hut's walls were hung with mirrors; each mirror was covered with a cloth. He asked Nzambi's daughter to uncover them so that he might see himself in them. She uncovered the first, and in it he saw the reflection of his own village. As she uncovered the others, he saw reflected all the villages he had passed through on his journey. But she refused to uncover the last one. "It shows the village from which no traveler returns," she said. But Mavungu insisted on seeing it. And then he said, "I must go there," and she could not dissuade him.

When Mavungu reached the village, he met a witch. He asked for fire to light his pipe, and she killed him. He just vanished into the air.

Now Luemba was getting worried about his brother, and decided to follow him. When he reached Nzambi's village, Nzambi himself rushed to meet him, shouting "Mavungu, you have returned!"

Luemba tried to explain that he was Mavungu's twin brother, but Nzambi would not listen, and took him straight to Mavungu's hut.

AFRICAN PIPES
Pipe smoking has long been popular with men and women in Africa. The evil old woman kills Mavungu when he is looking forward to a relaxing puff after his long journey.

Mavungu's twin brother, Luemba, finds and kills his brother's murderer

Luemba brings his brother back to life by touching his bones with his luck

That night, Luemba prayed to his luck and Mavungu's wife went straight to sleep still believing Luemba was her missing husband.

In the morning, Luemba saw the covered mirrors, and learned of the village from which no traveler returns. "I must go there," he said.

"What, again?" said Nzambi's daughter.

Luemba traveled to the village and encountered the witch. He asked her for fire and, before she could move, struck her dead.

Then Luemba gathered up his brother's bones, touched them with his luck, and they came back to life. Then the two brothers collected all the bones that lay scattered in that village of death, and each used their luck to bring them back to life. So now the two brothers had hundreds of devoted followers.

They returned to Nzambi's village, and then everyone could see that there were two brothers after all.

BROTHERLY HATE
This story of the Fjort people of Congo and Zaïre does not always end happily. Another ending tells that the brothers argued about their followers. Mavungu said they were his, because he was the elder; Luemba said they were his, because he had brought Mavungu back to life. Mavungu killed his brother, but Luemba's horse stayed with his body, touched him with his luck, and brought him back to life. Then Luemba rode after Mavungu and killed him. When the people heard the whole story, they all said that Luemba had done right.

An Eating Match with a Troll

MOUNTAIN KINGS
Norway's Dovrefjell
mountains are a famous
haunt of trolls and
fairies. Trolls vary in
temperament from kind
to evil, and in size from
gigantic to dwarfish.
Although they may
have more than one
head, they are not
usually very bright.
They avoid sunlight and
live in Scandinavian
mountain caves, where
they keep hoards of
treasure.

A POOR OLD FARMER had three idle sons. He was deep in debt, and sadly decided that the old wood his father had left him would have to be cut down and sold for firewood.

He told his eldest son to cut down the trees and the lad went off in a very bad temper. Deep in the wood he found a mossy old fir tree. As he raised his ax, the rumbling voice of a huge troll boomed, "This is my wood. If you chop down that tree, I will kill you!"

The lad dropped his ax and ran all the way home.

"You chicken," his father grumbled. "In my younger days, I would never have let a troll frighten me."

He sent his second son off to the wood and the same thing happened. The troll shouted; the boy ran.

"Who would have thought I could have sired two such fainthearts," cried the old farmer. "In my younger days, no troll would ever have stopped me from chopping down my own trees!" And, shaking his head, he sent his youngest son off to the wood.

This son was called the Ash Lad, because he spent all his time dozing by the fire.

"You'll soon be back with your tail between your legs," his brothers jeered.

"We'll see," the Ash Lad answered. He asked his mother to give him some cheese curds, which he put in a leather wallet around his waist.

To the troll's amazement, the lad squeezes water from a "stone"

When the Ash Lad came to the wood, the troll appeared, shouting. But the Ash Lad said, "Hold your noise, troll, or I'll squeeze the breath out of you like water from a stone."

"What do you mean, water from a stone?" asked the troll.

"This," said the Ash Lad. He took the curd cheese out of his wallet; it looked just like a white stone. He squeezed it in his fist, and clear whey spurted out.

Trolls aren't the most intelligent of creatures, and this one was frightened out of what wits he had. So the Ash Lad said, "If you help me cut down these trees, I'll not harm you."

When they had cut down all the trees, the troll invited the Ash Lad to supper. When they arrived at the troll's house, the troll helped himself to some water from two enormous iron pails. But the Ash Lad said, "There's not enough water in these finger-bowls to quench my thirst. Where's your spring? I'll go and fetch that."

The troll was more alarmed than ever. "Don't!" he blurted. "I need that spring! I'll fetch you as much water as you want."

Then the troll cooked a great cauldron of porridge. "The two of us will never eat all this," he said.

"Let's have an eating contest," cried the Ash Lad, and the troll agreed. The troll dug into the porridge with a huge spoon and so did the Ash Lad. But while the troll was eating, the Ash Lad was spooning his porridge into the leather wallet at his waist.

At last the troll said, "I'm so full I couldn't eat another mouthful."

"Same here," said the Ash Lad. "Let's make some room." And he took his knife and ripped a gash in the leather wallet, so that the porridge spilled out."

"Doesn't that hurt?" asked the troll.

"Not a bit," said the Ash Lad. "Why don't you try?"

The foolish troll took a knife to his belly and killed himself. And the Ash Lad took the troll's gold home to his father, who paid off all the family's debts with it.

GIANT KILLER
Similar events occur in the old English tale "Jack the Giant Killer," pictured above. Jack, like the Ash Lad, is the resourceful hero of a series of exciting, bloodthirsty battles with various giants. He defeats them all, saves King Arthur's kingdom from ruin, and rescues knights and ladies.

The Ash Lad appears to slit open his own stomach, letting the porridge spill out

The foolish troll tries the same trick – and kills himself. The lad escapes with the troll's treasure

The Ash Lad and the troll begin an eating contest

✍ Snow White ✍

ONCE UPON A TIME a queen sat sewing at a window. Snow was falling and some flakes landed on the window's ebony frame. Suddenly the queen pricked her finger with her needle and three drops of blood fell upon the snow. She said to herself, "If only I had a child as white as snow, as red as blood, and as black as ebony."

Soon afterward the queen had a daughter named Snow White, with skin white as snow, lips red as blood, and hair black as ebony. When she was born, the queen died.

After a year, the king remarried. The new queen was proud and vain. Every day she asked her magic mirror,

"Mirror, mirror, on the wall,
Who is the fairest of them all?"
And the mirror would reply,
"You are, O queen."

But one day, when Snow White was seven years old, the mirror replied, "Snow White is."

The spiteful queen told her huntsman, "Take Snow White into the forest and kill her. Bring me her liver and lungs as proof."

The huntsman took the child into the forest, but he hadn't the heart to kill her. He shot a young boar instead and took its lungs and liver to the queen. She had them made into a stew and ate them.

Snow White's mother

After Snow White's mother dies, a proud, vain beauty becomes queen

Alone and afraid, Snow White ran through the forest. At last she came to a cottage. Inside, on a table, were seven plates and cups, and upstairs were seven beds. Snow White ate from each plate, and drank from each cup. Then she lay down on each of the beds. Some were too long and some were too short, but the seventh was just right, and she lay down to sleep.

At nightfall, the owners of the cottage came home. They were seven dwarfs who mined silver in the mountains. First one and then the other asked, "Who's been eating from my plate?"

"Who's been drinking from my cup?"

"Who's been sleeping in my bed?"

Then the seventh dwarf looked in his bed and saw Snow White sleeping there. Not wanting to disturb her, he slept the night taking turns with the other six – one hour with each.

The next day Snow White told the dwarfs all about her stepmother

The dwarfs' cottage

Snow White happily agrees to cook and clean for the seven dwarfs

The huntsman

Disobeying the queen's orders, the huntsman spares Snow White and kills a wild boar instead

and the huntsman. They said, "If you'll take care of us, we'll take care of you."

So Snow White kept house for the seven dwarfs.

One day the queen asked her magic mirror,

DISNEY'S DWARFS
Walt Disney's *Snow White and the Seven Dwarfs* (1937) was the first full-length animated movie. One of Disney's most amusing touches was to give the dwarfs names reflecting their personalities: Grumpy, Sneezy, Doc, Bashful, Happy, Sleepy, and Dopey.

The old woman has pretty laces to sell

"Mirror, mirror, on the wall,
Who is the fairest of them all?"

"Snow White!" the mirror replied.

"So the child lives still," the jealous queen thought grimly. She disguised herself as an old woman selling brightly coloured laces and went from door to door searching for Snow White.

At last the queen arrived at the dwarfs' cottage. The dwarfs had told Snow White not to open the door to anyone, but she couldn't resist seeing the old woman's pretty laces.

The old woman said, "I'll lace you up." She laced Snow White up so tightly that she fainted.

The dwarfs take the poisoned comb from Snow White's hair and she comes back to life

THE TEMPTING APPLE
Offering an apple used to be a declaration of love. However the fruit is also linked with deceit and death. In this scene from Walt Disney's *Snow White*, the queen, transformed into a horrible hag, tempts Snow White with a poisoned apple.

"Now *I* am the fairest in the land once more," cackled the queen as she ran away.

When the dwarfs came home from the mines, they found Snow White. At first they thought she was dead, but when they cut her laces, she began to breathe, and soon she was herself again.

The next time the queen asked her mirror who was the fairest of them all, to her astonishment she once again received the answer, "Snow White." Disguised as an even older woman, she went back to the dwarfs' cottage.

This time, Snow White would not let her in. "Look at my pretty combs," the old woman said. Snow White leaned out of the window to see, and the old hag said, "Let me put this comb in your hair."

The comb was dipped in poison; as soon as it touched Snow White's hair, she fainted away.

That night, the dwarfs again thought Snow White was dead, but when they took the comb from her hair, she revived. They warned her to watch out for any more of her stepmother's tricks.

Meanwhile, the queen asked her mirror the question, and once again received the reply "Snow White". So, disguised as a farmer's wife, she went back to the cottage. She took with her a beautiful apple, white on one side and red on the other. However, the red side of the apple was poisoned.

Snow White would not let her in, but the old woman said, "Why not share my apple? I shall have the white side, and you shall have the red." As soon as Snow White bit into the apple, she fell dead. The queen laughed a cruel wicked laugh and walked away.

That night, the dwarfs tried everything, but they could not wake her. After weeping for three days, they put her in a glass coffin, with her name on it in golden letters: Princess Snow White.

They placed the glass coffin on top of a hill, and one of them was always there to grieve and watch over it. The birds, who had been

The old woman gives Snow White the poisoned half of the apple

very fond of Snow White, also came to weep for her: first an owl, then a raven, then a dove.

Snow White lay in her glass coffin, and as the years passed she grew into a young woman, her skin still white as snow, her lips red as blood, and her hair black as ebony.

One day, a prince came by. As soon as he saw Snow White, he fell in love with her. "Please let me have the coffin," he cried. "I'll pay you well for it!"

"We wouldn't sell it for the world," one of the dwarfs said.

"But I cannot live without Snow White!" sighed the prince.

SAD VIGIL
The dwarfs watch over Snow White in her glass coffin while she grows into a beautiful young woman in this 1903 German engraving by Alfred Zimmerman.

The seven dwarfs

A prince sees Snow White in her coffin and falls in love at first sight

The dwarfs relented and gave him the coffin. As his servants were carrying it, one of them stumbled, the coffin tilted, and the piece of poisoned apple fell from Snow White's mouth. At once she awoke. "Where am I?" she cried.

"Safe with me!" said the prince. "Live with me and be my queen!"

Everyone was invited to the wedding, even Snow White's stepmother. At first she thought she wouldn't go, but she couldn't resist. As soon as she arrived, the prince's guards seized her.

Iron slippers had been placed in the fire to get red hot. They were brought to her, and she stepped into them, and danced and danced until she dropped down dead.

The coffin tilts suddenly and Snow White awakes

The evil queen sees the red hot shoes and realizes her time has come

True Love Conquers All

In fairy tales, it is love, not money, rank, or power, that makes the world go round: a prince may wed the family servant, as in "Cinderella," or a witch's prisoner, as in "Rapunzel." Even those who proudly protest they will never marry are not safe from love's spell; their fate is to lose their hearts – not to humans – but to elusive fairies, such as the selkie or snow wife, and suffer inevitable sadness. For lovers, the road from "Once upon a time…" to "…happily ever after" can be long and hard, but, as stories like "The Black Bull of Norroway" and "The Snake Prince" make clear, there are no hardships or terrors that those inspired by true love cannot endure and eventually overcome.

The slipper fits Cinderella's foot – and the prince realizes that, despite her shabby clothes, she is his true love

Cinderella

ORIENTAL TALE
The most famous retelling of "Cinderella" is Charles Perrault's of 1697. He invented the fairy godmother, the pumpkin coach, and the glass slipper. The story originated in China, where a small foot was a mark of beauty. The first known version, "Yeh-hsien," dates from the 9th century AD.

ONCE UPON A TIME there was a man whose wife died, leaving him to bring up their only daughter; so he married again. His second wife was a sharp-tongued, stuck-up sort, and she had two daughters of her own who were just as bad. The man's own daughter was as gentle and good-natured as her mother had been.

It wasn't long before the stepmother and her two daughters began to make the poor girl's life miserable. They were always mean to her, and treated her just like a servant. The only place she could find any peace was in the chimney-corner, among the cinders: so they laughed at her and called her Cinderella. But Cinderella in rags was still far prettier than her stepsisters, for all their finery.

Now the king's son decided to give a ball, and he invited all the fine folk for miles around. There were to be two evenings of dancing and festivities. The sisters were thrilled. They could think and talk of nothing else, and they soon had Cinderella waiting on them hand and foot to make sure they looked their best. Cinderella even dressed their hair for them, and although she was as gentle as could be, they kept snapping, "Don't tug, girl," and "It's a good job you're not invited to the ball, you clumsy oaf!" Anyone else would have tangled their hair, but Cinderella was too kind-hearted for that.

When at last the sisters had squeezed themselves into their new dresses and set off for the ball, Cinderella sat down among the ashes, all alone. Then she began to cry.

When she looked up from her tears, an old lady was standing there. She had a kind face and was holding a wand in her hand. "Why are you crying?" she asked. "Tell me. I am your fairy godmother." So Cinderella told her godmother how much she longed to go to the ball.

"And so you shall," said her godmother. "Fetch me a pumpkin."

Cinderella's stepmother and stepsisters treat her like a servant

Cinderella went into the garden and picked the largest pumpkin she could find. Her godmother scooped out the insides, tapped it with her wand, and in an instant it had turned into a beautiful, gilded carriage. Then she looked in the mousetrap and found six live mice. When she touched them with her wand, they turned into six handsome dapple-gray horses.

The fairy godmother weaves her magic...

"Now we need a coachman," said the godmother, looking around for something suitable.

"I'll see if there is a rat in the rat trap," said Cinderella excitedly. There were three, and one of them had the finest whiskers you've ever seen. "He'd make a good coachman," said Cinderella. So her godmother tapped the rat with her wand, and he turned into a fat coachman with an enormous mustache.

...and turns a pumpkin into a coach, a fat rat into a coachman...

...six mice into horses...

...and six lizards into footmen in livery

"Now," said the godmother. "Behind the watering-can you will find six lizards. Bring them to me." When she tapped the lizards with her wand, they turned into six footmen, dressed in livery. "There – now you can go to the ball!"

"In these rags?" cried Cinderella.

So her godmother tapped Cinderella with her wand, and instantly her ragged clothes became a gown of silver and gold embroidered with pearls; and her worn-out shoes turned into glass slippers.

With a wave of her magic wand, the fairy godmother transforms Cinderella's rags into a ball gown fit for a princess

FAIRY GODMOTHER
Perrault's "fairy godmother" (shown above in a reversible drawing by Rex Whistler, c. 1935) is true to the spirit of earlier, oral versions, in which the Cinderella figure is helped by the spirit of her dead mother, sometimes in the form of a fish, a cow, or a tree.

BOX-OFFICE APPEAL
"Cinderella" has been adapted into a ballet (1945) with music by Sergei Prokoviev, and also into movies, as a Walt Disney cartoon (1950), and *The Slipper and the Rose* (1976), featured above.

As Cinderella climbed into the carriage her godmother told her, "Remember to leave the ball before midnight. For then the spell will end, and all these enchanted things will return to their true forms!"

When Cinderella arrived at the palace, no one could take their eyes off this beautiful stranger, who surely must be a princess. The prince himself danced with her all night. But at a quarter to twelve, she slipped out of the ballroom, and back to her carriage.

The next day the sisters were full of excited talk about the ball, and especially about the princess who had arrived so unexpectedly, and vanished so suddenly. Whoever could she be?

"Oh, I wish I could see her," said Cinderella. "Please, won't one of you lend me a dress – just an everyday one – so that I can go to the ball?"

"Certainly not!" said the sisters. "You'd disgrace us in front of the prince. And what would the lovely princess think, seeing us with a grubby creature like you?"

That night, when the sisters had left, Cinderella's fairy godmother transformed the pumpkin, rat, mice, and lizards again and sent her to the ball in her glass slippers and an even grander dress. "Don't forget to leave before midnight," she said.

At the ball, Cinderella and the prince soon fall in love

Cinderella and the prince danced together all night. They laughed and talked, and he whispered sweet nothings in her ear. She completely forgot the time. When she heard the chimes of midnight,

Cinderella fled. The prince ran after her, but all he found was one glass slipper. He questioned the palace guards, but they had not seen a princess leave – just a peasant girl.

Cinderella, meanwhile, made her own way home, with no carriage, no horses, no coachman, no servants, no fine dress. All that remained of her finery was a single glass slipper.

The prince, who was head over heels in love,

The clock strikes midnight and Cinderella has to flee

Cinderella

The prince finds Cinderella's glass slipper

The prince tries the slipper on Cinderella's foot and it fits perfectly, to the dismay of her stepmother and stepsisters

proclaimed that he would marry the girl whose foot fit the glass slipper. He visited every house in the kingdom in search of her.

At last the prince arrived at Cinderella's house. The two sisters tried as hard as they could to squeeze their big feet into the glass slipper, but in vain. "Is there no other girl in the house?" asked the prince.

"No," the sisters replied. "Unless you count Cinderella, but she's just a grimy little good-for-nothing."

"Nevertheless," said the prince, "let her try on the slipper."

So Cinderella came out from the chimney-corner. Her foot slid as neatly into the glass slipper as a sword into its sheath. As she stood there, in her tattered dress all smeared with dust and ashes, the prince still thought she was the most beautiful girl in the world.

So Cinderella and the prince were married and lived happily ever after. And Cinderella, who was as good as she was beautiful, forgave her sisters and took them to live with her in the palace, where they married two great lords of the court.

GRIMM ENDING
In the Grimms' version of "Cinderella," the stepsisters each cut a piece from one foot to make it fit the slipper. Their attempts to fool the prince are thwarted by two pigeons cooing:
"Turn and peep, turn and peep,
There's blood within the shoe,
The shoe it is too small for her,
The true bride waits for you."
Later, at Cinderella's wedding, the same pigeons peck the sisters' eyes out!

131

Rapunzel

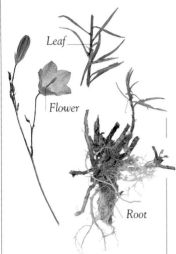

RAMPION
"Rapunzel" is the German for rampion, a type of harebell with delicate blue flowers. Its first-year roots and young leaves can be used in salads.

A MAN AND WIFE yearned for a child and at last God granted their wish. One day the wife was standing at a window looking down on the garden of their neighbor, who was a witch. The garden, which was full of flowers, herbs, and vegetables, was surrounded by a high wall. The wife gazed longingly at a bed of fresh green rapunzel and called out to her husband, "I must have some of that rapunzel or I will die."

At dusk her husband climbed the garden wall, snatched a handful of rapunzel, and took it to her. She ate it greedily, but it tasted so good that her craving grew. She now wanted rapunzel more than ever. Once again her husband crept into the witch's garden. But this time the witch was waiting.

The witch catches her next-door neighbor stealing rapunzel from her garden

HERB GARDEN
This 14th-century book illustration shows a doctor selecting herbs in an herb garden. At that time, herbs were much more important for medicinal purposes than for cooking, and anyone specializing in making medicines or potions – a witch, for example – would be likely to maintain a well-stocked herb garden.

"How dare you steal my rapunzel?" she hissed. "You'll pay for this!"

"Have mercy," begged the man. "My wife saw your rapunzel from our window, and said she would die if she did not have some!"

"If what you say is true," the witch replied, "take as much rapunzel as you like. But on one condition: when your wife gives birth, you must give me the child." The terrified man agreed, and, when a baby girl was born, the witch carried her off.

"Her name shall be Rapunzel," she said.

Rapunzel grew to be the loveliest child under the sun. When she was twelve, the witch took her into the forest and shut her in a tower that had neither stairs nor door, only a window at the top. When the witch wanted to come in, she stood below and shouted, "Rapunzel, Rapunzel, let down your hair!" Rapunzel had long, long hair, fine as spun gold, and, when she heard the witch's cry, she would unfasten her braids, twist them around the window hooks, and let her tresses fall to the ground for the witch to climb up.

A few years later, the king's son chanced to ride through the forest. As he passed the tower, he heard a voice singing so sweetly that he had to stop and listen. The prince longed to see the owner of the voice, but the tower had neither door nor stairs, so he rode home. But every day he returned to listen.

One day the prince was standing behind a tree when the witch arrived and he heard her call, "Rapunzel, Rapunzel, let down your hair!"

Rapunzel undid her braids, and the witch climbed the ladder of golden hair. "So that's how it's done," he thought. The next day he came to the tower and called, "Rapunzel, Rapunzel, let down your hair!"

She did so and the prince climbed up. Rapunzel had never seen a man before, but the prince spoke so gently to her that she soon lost her fear. He told her that he had been captivated by her singing and couldn't rest until he had seen her. And then he asked if she would be his bride.

She saw that he was young and handsome and thought, "He will love me more than my old godmother does." So she answered yes, and put her hand in his. "Bring a skein of silk with you every time you come," she added. "I can weave a ladder from it. When it is done I shall climb down and ride away with you."

The witch hides Rapunzel in a high tower

The tower

When the witch visits Rapunzel, she tells her to let down her hair

The prince

The prince sees the witch climb up tresses of golden hair

When the prince reaches the top of the tower, he is captivated by Rapunzel's beauty

DARK FORESTS
Over a quarter of Germany is forest, and for centuries forests such as this one in north-eastern Germany have provided suitably atmospheric settings for the country's rich store of fairy tales and legends. The dense forest in "Rapunzel" cuts the heroine off from the outside world. Only when she escapes it does she find happiness.

After several years apart, Rapunzel and the blind prince meet again in her desert home

They agreed that he should visit her every evening, for the old witch came only by day. The witch suspected nothing, until one morning Rapunzel asked her, "Godmother, why is it that my dresses no longer fit?" For she had fallen pregnant to her husband, the prince.

"Wicked child!" cried the witch. "I thought I had shut you away from the world, but you have deceived me!" In her anger, she cut off Rapunzel's beautiful hair – snip! snip! Then she took Rapunzel out into a desert, and left her there.

That evening, when the prince came to the tower and called, "Rapunzel, Rapunzel, let down your hair," the witch lowered the cut braids. The prince climbed up.

"Aha!" glowered the witch. "The bird has flown the nest. She won't be singing any more; the cat has got her. And the same cat will scratch your eyes out. You will never see your Rapunzel again!"

Determined to trap the prince, the witch cuts off Rapunzel's golden hair

In despair, the prince leaped from the tower. As he fell, thorns scratched his eyes and made him blind. He stumbled away, weeping.

The prince wandered for several years, until at last he came to the desert where Rapunzel was living with the twins she had borne – a boy and girl. He heard a voice sweetly singing, and when he came closer, Rapunzel recognized him. She hugged him close and wept, and as she wept two tears fell on his eyes and his eyesight returned.

The prince took Rapunzel and their children back to his kingdom, where they were welcomed with joy, and lived in happiness and contentment.

Rapunzel's children

❧ The Heart's Door ❧

ONCE THERE WAS a young man named Severi who set out to seek his fortune. He walked over hills and meadows, and through deep woods, until at last he came to the sea. There he saw a little rowboat on the shore.

Severi got into the boat and set out across the ocean. The boat was tossed by the winds and lashed by the rains and at last a huge wave washed Severi overboard. But he did not lose heart. He swam night and day until he reached a white beach at the foot of a black cliff. Dangling from the cliff top was a rope, so Severi climbed up.

At the top of the cliff Severi found a path that led him down into the heart of the hill. At the bottom he came to a golden door, which opened for him. He stepped through into a magic world of green meadows, beautiful flowers, and trees hung with golden fruit.

There Severi met an old man with long white hair who asked him who he was and where he was going. "My name is Severi," he replied, "but I do not know where I am going."

"Then stay here," said the old man, "and be my servant."

So Severi went to live with the old man in his copper castle.

The next morning the old man said that he must go away on a long journey. "Here are the keys to the castle," he said. "There are twenty-four keys for twenty-four rooms. Feel free to go into all the rooms except the last. If you go in there, you go at your own risk."

When Severi was left alone in the castle, he began to explore the twenty-three rooms. Each one was more wonderful than the last. One was all gold, another all silver, another black ebony, another polished marble. But at last he had seen all of them, and then he was sad. "Now all my adventures are over," he said. "There's nothing left to see. I might as well go home."

But when he woke up the next morning, Severi found the key to the twenty-fourth room clutched tight in his hand. "It's a sign," he thought. "I shall open the twenty-fourth door, and take the risk."

MAGICAL CASTLE
Though built of stone, not copper like the one described in this story, Olavinlinna's lakeland setting helps make it one of Finland's most impressive castles. Situated in Savonlinna in the east of the country, it dates from 1475.

Severi steps into a magical, enchanted world

135

Severi sees Vappu, the loveliest girl in the world, sitting on a golden throne

When he opened the last door, he saw in the middle of the room a high throne, and sitting on it was the loveliest girl in the whole world.

"Who are you?" asked Severi.

"My name is Vappu," said the girl, "and I have been waiting for you for the longest time." Her voice rippled through the air like the notes of a harp.

Severi and Vappu lived happily together in the copper castle for a whole month. They used to sit by the silver stream and feast on the golden fruit from the old man's garden with never a care in the world. But one day they fell asleep beside the stream, and when Severi awoke, Vappu was gone.

Severi called and called for her. "Vappu! Vappu!" But the only answer was the twittering of the red and golden birds that flitted through the trees.

GOLDEN DAYS
Summer is short in Finland, but for about four weeks the sun never sets and the countryside is transformed into something like the golden paradise described in this tale. Then, like a door closing, winter returns.

Vappu vanishes, but the old man's magic brings her back. To keep her, Severi must win a game of hide and seek. The old man whispers a magic spell

The old man came home to find Severi deep in misery. "I warned you not to open the twenty-fourth door," he said.

"I am man enough to make my own choices," replied Severi.

"And now you have made them, are you wiser for it?"

"My sorrow has made me older," said Severi, "and wiser, too."

Then the old man muttered a magic spell, and Vappu reappeared, radiant as a sunbeam.

"Never leave me again!" said Severi.

"I will not," said Vappu, "on one condition. You must hide from me so that I cannot find you. I will give you three chances."

Severi did not know how to outwit clever Vappu, but the old man whispered a magic charm to him that he said would help.

First Severi hid among the wild rabbits, but Vappu tracked him down. Then Severi tried to hide among the wild bears, but Vappu tracked him down.

At last, Severi resolved to hide in Vappu's heart. He said,

"Three times I knock at your door, dear heart.

Let me in, heart's jewel, let me in."

Vappu looked all around. "It is strange," she said. "One minute Severi was standing beside me. Now he is gone."

So Severi called to her, "Can you not find me, my golden one?"

"No, I cannot," said Vappu. "Where are you?"

"I am here, in your heart," said Severi.

FIRESIDE STORY
In Finland, fairy tales were traditionally told around the fire in a tupa, a peasant's hut. This story's beautiful imagery would have cheered listeners on long winter nights.

He hides among the rabbits and hides among the bears. Each time Vappu finds him

"Then my heart is yours," said Vappu.

Severi came out from her heart, and the two lovers embraced. They lived happily ever after in the copper castle in that kingdom, beside the silver stream, beneath the golden trees.

Then he finds the perfect place to hide – in her heart

The Goodman of Wastness

ISLAND OF SELKIES

There are many selkie stories in Orkney and Shetland, an area well known for seals. Wastness may well be modern-day Westness, on the coast of the Orkney island of Rousay. A similar Irish tale tells of a man who captures a beautiful, green-haired merrow, a sea fairy, by stealing her magic diving cap.

MERMAID
Similar to the selkie, and also with a sweet singing voice, is the mermaid (above), which, according to the accounts of lonely sailors, has a woman's head and body and a fish's tail.

THE GOODMAN OF WASTNESS was a handsome bachelor. All the girls of Orkney set their caps at him, but he would have none of them. "I'm happy as I am," he said.

One day the goodman went walking by the sea. There he saw a band of the selkie folk, the seal people who live in the ocean in those parts. They were naked, having set aside their seal skins in the warm sun. They were playing and laughing, and diving off rocks into the sea. But although the water was deep enough for diving on the ocean side, on the shore side it was just a shallow pool. The goodman crept through this pool and snatched one of the skins.

The selkies grabbed their skins and fled. They swam out to sea and turned to stare at the man who had dared to sneak up on them. Each head was the head of a seal, except for one.

The goodman walked away. He was not even back on dry land before he heard a girl sobbing and pleading

The goodman seizes the selkie's seal skin, and she is forced to follow him

behind him. It was the poor girl whose skin he had taken. "Man, if there is any mercy in you, give me back my skin!" she begged. "I cannot, cannot, cannot live in the sea without it. I cannot, cannot, cannot live with my own folk without a seal skin. Have pity on me, as you hope for pity yourself."

Now the goodman did indeed pity the girl, but no sooner did he feel pity than he also felt love. And of the two emotions, love was the stronger. So he kept the skin. He argued, and higgled, and haggled, until the girl agreed to marry him and live on the land.

So they were married and in time the sea-girl bore her husband seven children, four boys and three girls. She had a laugh that rippled like the waves of the sea and you might have thought her happy. But when no one was watching, she used to gaze out to sea, and she taught her children mournful songs that nobody had ever heard the like of before.

In all this time, she had had never so much as an inkling of where her seal skin might be hidden. One day, the goodman took his three oldest boys fishing, and the wife sent three of the other children to collect whelks on the seashore. Only the youngest girl stayed at home, because she had a sore foot. As soon as the others were gone, the wife began to search the house, as she did every time she was left alone. She looked everywhere; but she couldn't find the seal skin.

The goodman marries the mysterious selkie and in time they have seven children

The youngest child tells where her father hid the selkie's seal skin

"What are you looking for?" asked her youngest.

"For a seal skin to wrap up your sore foot."

"I know where it is," said the girl. "I once saw father take one down from the space between the wall and the roof. He looked at it a minute, then put it back."

The wife rushed to the place and pulled down her long-lost skin. "Farewell, peerie buddo!" she cried. "Farewell, little darling!" She ran to the beach, put on the seal skin, and dived into the sea.

The goodman was coming home in his fishing boat as a seal swam past him. It was his wife. She uncovered her face and sang:

"Goodman of Wastness, farewell to thee!
I liked you well, you were good to me,
But better I love my man of the sea!"

He never saw his beautiful seal-wife again.

The selkie wife puts on her skin and joyfully returns to the sea, leaving husband and children behind

The Snake Prince

ONCE IN A CITY in India there lived a poor old woman who had nothing to eat but a little dry flour. She took a brass pot down to the river to collect water to mix with the flour so she could make some bread.

She left the brass pot on the bank while she bathed. A little later when she came to fill it with water, she lifted the cloth cover and saw inside the glittering coils and flicking tongue of a deadly snake!

She replaced the cloth, saying, "Better to die from snakebite than hunger. I will take you home, shake you from the pot, and then all my troubles shall be at an end."

But when she upturned the pot on her hearthstone, instead of a snake, out fell a necklace of flashing jewels.

The old woman took the magnificent necklace to the rajah, who rewarded her with enough money to keep her in comfort for the rest of her life.

Soon afterward the rajah was invited by a neighboring rajah to celebrate the birth of a baby girl. The rajah said to his wife, the rani, "Now is your chance to wear that beautiful necklace." The rani went to her jewel chest to fetch the necklace, but when she opened the lid, instead of a necklace, she found a fat little baby boy, crowing and shouting. The rani, who had no children of her own, picked him up, crying, "You are more precious than any necklace."

GREEN FIRE
The necklace in the tale could have resembled this one, made of emeralds and enameled gold sections. Called a *satratana*, each of its seven jewels represents a planet in Indian astrology.

The old woman

After bathing in the river, the old woman finds a snake in her brass pot

She takes the necklace to the rajah, who rewards her

The necklace turns into a baby boy, who becomes the rajah's son

So the rajah sent to his neighbor, and said that he could not come, for he must celebrate the birth of his own baby boy.

In time, it was arranged that the two children should marry and, when they were grown, the wedding took place with much rejoicing. But the neighboring rajah and rani had heard rumors that there was something odd about the prince's birth. They told their daughter not to speak a word to her husband after the wedding. "When he asks you what is the matter," urged her mother, "tell him you will never speak to him unless he tells you the secret of his birth."

After the wedding, the prince begged his wife to speak to him.

"Tell me the secret of your birth," she said.

He replied, "If I did, you would regret it till the end of your life."

And so the days passed in brooding silence. The prince's secret lay between man and wife like a cloud between the sun and the earth.

At last the prince could bear it no longer. "At midnight you shall have your wish," he said. "But I warn you, you will regret it." His wife paid no heed to his warnings.

At midnight, they rode down to the river, where the old woman had gone with her brass pot. The prince said, "Do you still insist on learning my secret?"

"Yes!" answered his wife.

"Then," said the prince, "know that I am the son of the king of a far country, who was turned by enchantment into a sna..."

GREAT KING
Each Indian state was once ruled by a rajah (king), whose wife was called a rani. One of the most powerful was the Maharajah of Lahore (above).

The prince marries a princess – who refuses to speak until he tells her the secret of his birth

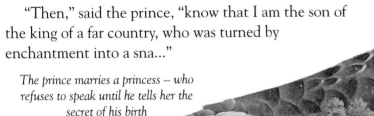

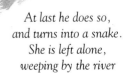

At last he does so, and turns into a snake. She is left alone, weeping by the river

DOWN BY THE RIVER
This fine view of the
Yamuna River, with the
Taj Mahal in the
background, conjures
up the riverside setting
of this tale.

Even as the prince said the fateful word, he turned back into a snake and slid into the river. By the light of the moon, the princess saw ripples on the black water as the snake swam away. And then she was alone on the riverbank.

The princess wept and tore her clothes. She ordered her servants to build her a little house of black stone by the river, and there she lived, mourning for her lost husband.

A long time passed. Then one day, when the princess awoke, she saw a trail of fresh mud on the carpet of her bedroom. She summoned her guards, but they swore that no one had entered. The next night, the same thing happened. On the third night, the princess was determined to stay awake. She took a knife, cut her hand, and rubbed salt into the wound so the pain would keep her from sleeping.

At midnight, a snake slithered into her room, leaving a trail of mud at it went. It crawled toward her bed, raised its flat head onto the mattress and stared at her.

"Who are you? What do you want?" she whispered, trembling with fear.

The princess mourns the loss of her prince in her house of black stone

Because of the pain of her cut hand, the princess is wide awake when her snake husband slithers to her bedside at midnight

FRONTIER TALE
This story comes from
Firozpûr, on the Indian
side of the border with
Pakistan.

The snake replied, "I am your husband." The princess began to weep. The snake continued, "Did I not tell you that if you forced my secret from me, you would regret it?"

"I do regret it," she said. "I regret it every day. If only there was something I could do to make things right again."

"There is something," said the snake, "but it is very dangerous. Tomorrow night, place a large bowl of milk and sugar in each of the four corners of this room. All the snakes in the river will come to drink, and the one that leads the way will be the queen of snakes. You must bar her way at the door and say, 'Queen of snakes, queen of snakes, give me back my husband!' If you show no fear, you will win my freedom. But if you flinch, you will never see me again."

That night the princess put out the bowls of milk and sugar and waited. At midnight she heard a great hissing from the river, and soon the whole riverbank was seething with snakes. At their head was a huge hooded creature with gleaming, shimmering scales.

The princess's guards ran in terror.

The guards

The princess bravely faces the snakes, and wins back her husband

SERPENT GODS
Snakes are especially important in Hindu culture as symbols of fertility. Semidivine creatures called *nagas* (above, a 12th-century bronze), half human, half snake, inhabit bejeweled palaces in underworld kingdoms. They are associated with water, especially wells, rivers, and lakes.

But the princess stood in the doorway and commanded, "Queen of snakes, give me back my husband."

The rustling, writhing snakes seemed to hiss "Husssband! Husssband!"

The snake queen's head swayed to and fro, fixing the princess with wicked, beady eyes. But the princess did not flinch. "Queen of snakes, give me back my husband," she repeated.

The snakes, led by their queen, crawl from the river

"Tomorrow!" said the snake queen. "Tomorrow!"

Then the princess stood aside, and the snakes flooded into her room, jostling greedily over the bowls of sweet milk.

The next morning the princess dressed in her most beautiful sari. She filled the house with flowers and waited. At midnight, the prince came walking through the door and they fell into each other's arms. There were never any secrets between them again.

WINDOW DRESSING
This woman, like the princess at the end of this tale, is dressed in her "most beautiful sari." She is sitting in a window of the Jaisalamer Palace, Rajasthan, India.

Falling Star

CAMPFIRE STORY
This Native American tale is especially popular among the Cheyenne, who once pitched their buffalo-hide tepees (above) on the vast North American plains.

UP A TREE
In this story, Brightest Star takes on the form of a porcupine to lure First Girl up into the sky world. Porcupine meat is edible, which helps explain why First Girl pursues it. The North American porcupine frequently climbs pine trees to feed on bark.

ONE SUMMER'S NIGHT two girls lay outside their tepee looking up at the stars. "Look at that one!" said First Girl. "It's the brightest of them all. I would like to marry that star."

The next day the two girls were gathering wood when they saw a porcupine climbing a tree.

"I'll fetch him down," said First Girl, scrambling up the tree after him. The porcupine kept climbing, always just out of reach, but First Girl kept climbing, too.

"Come down! Come down!" begged Second Girl, but soon First Girl was too high to hear.

The pine tree went up and up until it reached the sky world. First Girl began to weep with fear because she had climbed so high. Then a voice said, "Don't cry. I am Brightest Star, and I would like to marry you."

So First Girl and Brightest Star were married. Brightest Star said that she could do anything she liked in the sky world, but if she dug up any of the white turnips that grew there, something bad was sure to happen.

They lived happily together, and soon had a child. But First Girl couldn't help being curious about the white turnips and one day she dug one up. It left a hole in the sky world through which she could see the earth far below. Longing to see her home again, she wove some grass into a rope. It looked long enough to reach the ground, so First Girl began to climb down through the hole, her baby in her arms.

She is met at the top by Brightest Star

She follows a porcupine up a tree

First Girl longs to marry the brightest star

144

First Girl longs to visit her home on earth

She climbs down with her baby, but the rope is too short and she falls

The boy soon learns to run as fast as the larks fly

The baby is rescued by a meadowlark

But when First Girl reached the end of the rope, the ground was still far below her. She clung on desperately, but at last her strength gave out and she fell…

She died, but her baby, who was made of star-stone, survived. A meadowlark carried the child to her nest, and took care of him alongside her own fledglings. She called him Falling Star.

The boy grew quickly and could soon run fast enough to keep up with the flying birds. But the meadowlark was sad he had no wings. When winter approached, and it was time for the larks to fly south, she knew he could not make such a long journey on foot.

"Make me a bow and arrows, and I will look after myself," said Falling Star.

With the bow and arrows the larks made for him, he walked along a river, and so came to the tepees of his mother's people. He said to an old woman there, "Grandmother, I am thirsty."

"I can't give you water," she replied. "There's a monster in the river that swallows up anyone who goes near!"

But Falling Star's throat was so parched he borrowed her bucket of buffalo skin and her buffalo-horn ladle and went to the river. As soon as he dipped the ladle in the water, an enormous monster reared up, opened its gaping mouth, and sucked him down.

SHARPSHOOTER
The bow and arrow was the Cheyenne's principal weapon. Arrows were tipped with buffalo bone; a hide quiver, decorated with dyed porcupine quills, held about 20. The bow was of hardwood, and only about 3 ft (1 m) long, making it easy to use on horseback. The bowstring was a twisted buffalo sinew.

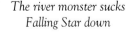

The river monster sucks Falling Star down

BUFFALO HUNTING
The Cheyenne
depended on the buffalo
(above) that once
roamed the plains for
food, tools, and hides.
Before the Cheyenne
acquired horses, they
used to sneak up on a
herd by disguising
themselves as animals –
as Falling Star does in
this story.

*Disguised as a buffalo,
Falling Star catches the
white crow*

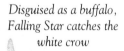

The fast runners

Inside the creature's stomach, crouched in fear at the back, Falling Star found all the other people the monster had swallowed alive.

Falling Star's mother was a Cheyenne girl, but his father was a star, and he was made of star-stone. He punched a hole in the monster's side and killed it. The

*Falling Star punches a hole in the
monster's side*

people crawled out, and Falling Star took them back to the camp.

Then Falling Star went to the old woman and said, "Grandmother, I am hungry."

She replied, "I cannot give you any food. Whenever the men go out to hunt, a white crow warns the buffalo that they are coming."

"Do not worry about that," said Falling Star. "Bring me a buffalo skin and two fast runners."

He said to the fast runners, "You must pretend to shoot me."

Falling Star put on the old buffalo skin and joined the buffalo herd. When the two runners approached, the white crow flew up, calling, "Run! Hunters are coming!" The buffalo herd ran away, with Falling Star in his shabby old skin following behind. The runners shot their arrows, and Falling Star fell down as if he were dead. The white crow circled above him, calling, "Why were you so slow?" The crow flew closer and closer. Falling Star reached out from beneath the buffalo skin and caught it by the legs.

He carried the bird back to the camp in triumph and presented it to the chief, who announced, "I will take this bird to my tepee, tie him to the smoke hole, and smoke him to death."

From that day on, the Cheyennes were able to kill as many buffalo as they needed, and never went hungry.

The people were so grateful that they gave Falling Star a fine tepee of his own and the prettiest girl in the tribe for his bride.

And every night, Brightest Star, Falling Star's father, shone down from the sky, and blessed them with his light.

❧ The Snow Wife ❧

LONG AGO there was a young man who had never found a girl he wanted to marry, so he lived alone. One winter night, during a violent snowstorm, he heard a knock at his door. When he opened it, he found a young woman lying in a heap outside.

He brought her into the house, and soon she began to revive, though her face remained as pale as snow. She was so beautiful that he asked her to become his wife.

The young man carries the girl inside, and she revives

LAND OF SNOW
The story of the Snow Wife is very popular in various versions in Japan, particularly in the west, where the snow often lies many feet deep and may remain on the ground for up to six months.

They lived happily together all that winter, but as the spring thaws approached and the weather grew warmer, the young wife began to lose her strength. She grew thinner and weaker every day.

The young man thought that perhaps his wife was pining for company, so he asked some friends to a party to celebrate the coming of spring. In the middle of the party, while the guests were eating and drinking, the young man called out to his wife in the kitchen. When she did not answer, he went to look for her.

She was nowhere to be seen. There was only her kimono, lying in a pool of water in front of the stove.

To his dismay, he finds only her kimono and a pool of water

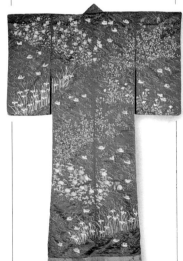

SILK KIMONO
When spring comes, the Snow Wife melts away, leaving only her beautiful kimono behind. This traditional robe, like the one shown above, would have been made of embroidered silk.

The Sleeping Prince

A KING HAD A DAUGHTER who was his heart's delight. When he had to go to war, he worried what would become of her. "Go well, father, and return well," she said. "I shall be waiting."

Every day she sat at her window, watching for her father's return and embroidering a handkerchief to give him. One day a golden eagle wheeled across the sky, calling, "Embroider away, embroider away; you shall marry a dead man one day."

"What do you mean?" asked the princess.

"Climb on my back and you shall see," the eagle replied.

The eagle carried her far away, to a courtyard where stood a well. The princess looked into the well; at the bottom was a palace.

There she found a prince lying as if dead. A note by his side read, "If you pity me, watch over me for three months, three weeks, three hours, and three minutes. When I sneeze, say 'Bless you, my prince, may you live forever.' I shall wake and claim you as my bride."

The princess sat by the sleeping prince for three months and three weeks. Food was brought to her, but she never saw anyone bring it and she had no one to talk to. So when she heard a girl calling "Serving maid for hire!" from outside the well, she called back, "Look down the well!"

An eagle carries the princess far away – to a palace at the bottom of a well

BIG BIRDS
Fairy-tale eagles, like the one in this story, are often hugely powerful – none more so than the rocs of *The Arabian Nights*, illustrated above by J. D. Batten in 1895.

The maid

For months the princess watches over the sleeping prince – then she hears a voice calling "Serving maid for hire!"

The girl looked pretty and kind and the princess hired her as her maid. She told her all about the sleeping prince. The maid said, "Go to sleep. I will keep watch and wake you if the prince sneezes."

As soon as the princess fell asleep, the prince sneezed. Quick as a flash the maid said, "Bless you, my prince, may you live forever."

The prince awoke and embraced the maid.

"You have freed me from a magic spell," he said. "You shall be my bride." Then he noticed the princess asleep on the floor.

"That's my maid," said the maid.

"Let the poor thing sleep," smiled the prince. "Then send her out to mind the geese."

When the princess awoke, her maid told her, "The prince woke up, and said he wanted me, not you, and you were to mind the geese."

There was nothing the princess could do.

The prince asked the maid what gift she would like. "A crown of diamonds," she replied. He asked the goose girl what she would like. She replied, "The millstone of patience, the hangman's rope, and the butcher's knife." He gave each girl what she asked for.

That night the prince heard sad murmurings coming from the goose girl's room. The princess was

The princess is unfairly sent to mind the geese

As soon as the princess falls asleep, the prince sneezes and finds the maid

The princess

The maid

The prince

Crown

Millstone

Knife

Rope

The prince bursts into the room, just in time to stop the lovelorn princess from killing herself out of grief

telling the millstone of patience her troubles. She asked, "Millstone, what should I do?"

"Have patience," the millstone replied.

Then she asked the knife, "Knife, what should I do?"

"Stab yourself!" the knife replied.

Then she asked the rope, "Rope, what should I do?"

"Hang yourself!" the rope replied.

The prince burst in. "Don't do it!" he shouted. "You are my true bride and that other girl is a liar. It is she who should hang!"

"No," said the princess. "Though she tried to do me harm, let her go free. Just take me home to my father and marry me."

GOOD NIGHT, PRINCE! The story of the sleeping prince is particularly popular in Greece, and is also found in Italy and Armenia.

149

Ivan & the Firebird

DANCE OF FIRE
Russian folklore has many other Firebird tales, one of which formed the basis of the world-famous ballet with music by Igor Stravinsky. It was first performed in Paris in 1910 with costumes designed by Leon Bakst.

GOLDEN ORIOLE
A glittering yellow feather from the golden oriole, a shy bird that inhabits woodland across Europe and central Asia, may have helped inspire the legend of the magical Firebird.

Ivan spies the Firebird's golden feather

ONCE THERE LIVED a mighty czar, who had in his service a brave young huntsman named Ivan, the owner of a magic talking horse. One day when Ivan was riding through the forest, he spied a golden feather, shining like a flame, lying on the path. It was a feather from the Firebird.

"Leave that feather alone!" said Ivan's horse. "If you pick it up, you'll pick up trouble with it." But Ivan was not afraid of trouble, so he picked up the feather and gave it to the czar.

"This feather is so lovely," the czar declared, "that I must have the whole bird. If I can't have the Firebird, you shall lose your head."

Ivan went to his horse and wept bitter tears. The horse said, "I told you so. But don't cry yet. The *real* trouble is still to come. Go to the czar and ask to have a hundred sacks of corn scattered over a field."

Ivan did so, and the next day at dawn he rode out to the field and hid behind a tree. As the sun rose, he heard a rustling like the waves of the sea. It was the Firebird's wings. As it alighted on the corn, the horse came forward and stepped on its wing. Ivan bound it tightly with cords and brought it to the czar.

The czar was delighted with this gift and made Ivan a nobleman. But then he said, "Since you were so clever at catching the Firebird, you shall fetch me a bride. Beyond three times nine lands, at the edge of the world, lives the princess Vasilisa. Bring her to me and I will make you rich. Fail and you will lose your head!"

The Firebird alights on the scattered corn; Ivan catches it for the czar

Ivan

Ivan's magic talking horse

Ivan went back to the horse, weeping bitter tears. The horse said, "I told you so. But don't cry yet. The *real* trouble is still to come. Go to the king and ask him for a tent with a golden roof and provisions for the journey."

After that, Ivan mounted his magic horse and rode off across three times nine lands to the edge of the world, where the red sun rises in flames from the deep blue sea. He stopped on the golden sand and looked out to sea. There he saw Princess Vasilisa rowing a silver boat with golden oars.

EDGE OF THE WORLD
Ivan's journey to the "edge of the world" might have taken him to Provideniya Bay (above) on Russia's east coast.

Where the grasslands met the sand, Ivan set up his golden-roofed tent, laid out a feast from the wonderful provisions the czar had given him, and settled down to wait for the the princess.

When Princess Vasilisa saw the golden roof of the tent, she rowed toward the shore. As she stepped from her boat, Ivan said, "Welcome! Please be my guest and taste the fine wines I have brought from foreign lands."

The princess entered the tent, and soon she and Ivan were deep in talk and laughter as they ate and drank the czar's wonderful food and wine. After a while, she became sleepy. As soon as she had fallen asleep, Ivan folded up the tent, mounted the magic horse, and, with the sleeping princess lying across the saddle, set off for home like an arrow shot from a bow.

The czar was overjoyed to see the princess. He rewarded Ivan with gold and silver and made him even more noble than before. But when Princess Vasilisa awoke, and found that she was pledged in marriage to the wicked old czar, she was grief-stricken.

When Ivan first sees Princess Vasilisa, she is rowing a silver boat with golden oars

Obeying the czar's orders, Ivan carries off the sleepy princess

The cruel, greedy czar is overjoyed to see the princess, but she is grief-stricken

THE CZARS
The word czar comes from Caesar, the name adopted by the Roman emperors. The czars ruled the Russian Empire from 1547 to the Russian Revolution of 1917. Among the most ruthless were Ivan the Terrible and Peter the Great (above). They were absolute rulers, with total power over their subjects, like the czar in this tale.

CUNNING CRAB
The crab has a reputation for deviousness in many cultures – perhaps because of its sideways, scuttling walk. In this story, however, a well-placed hoof prevents any sneaky crab tricks!

Nothing the czar could say would bring back her smile. She said, "I will never marry except in my wedding gown, and that is hidden beneath a stone in the middle of the deep blue sea."

The czar said to Ivan, "Fetch Princess Vasilisa's wedding gown. Or you shall lose your head."

Ivan went to his horse and wept bitter tears. The horse said, "I told you so. But don't cry yet. The *real* trouble is still to come. Climb up and I will take you to the sea."

When they reached the sea, the horse stepped on a huge crab that was crawling out of the ocean. The crab said, "Spare me, please! I will do whatever you want."

Ivan said, "Fetch me the wedding gown of Princess Vasilisa, which is underneath a stone in the middle of the deep blue sea."

The crab gave a harsh cry and the sea began to heave. From it crawled thousands of crabs, ready to do their king's bidding. He sent them down into the depths of the ocean. In an hour they returned with the princess's wedding gown.

Ivan brought the gown to the czar, who said, "Now, Princess Vasilisa, will you marry me?"

The crab king

Ivan asks the king of the crabs to fetch Princess Vasilisa's wedding gown from the depths of the sea. Thousands of little crabs do their king's bidding

"I will only marry you," said the princess, "if you order Ivan to jump into a vat of boiling water."

The czar was so eager to marry the princess that, despite everything Ivan had done for him, he ordered a cauldron of water to be set over a fire and brought to the boil. And when it was boiling, he ordered it to be brought forward.

This is the trouble my horse warned me of, thought Ivan. If only I had listened to him! Then Ivan said to the czar, "Please let me say farewell to my faithful horse." The czar nodded, and Ivan went to the magic horse and flung his arms around its neck.

"Why are you crying?" asked the horse.

"The czar wants me to be boiled alive," wept Ivan.

"Do not cry yet. There are worse troubles than this," said the horse,

The princess says she will only marry the czar if Ivan is boiled alive

By his horse's magic, the boiling water makes Ivan even more handsome!

HUBBLE BUBBLE
The cauldron is a powerful symbol of magical transformation, fertility, and rebirth. In past times, a cauldron was an essential part of a witch or wizard's equipment. The one in this tale has magic powers of renewal – but only for the hero.

Ivan says farewell to his faithful steed

Believing the boiling water will make him young and good-looking, the old czar jumps in the cauldron

WICKED WIZARD
The villain of other Firebird stories, replacing this tale's greedy czar, is an evil wizard named Koschei the Deathless, here illustrated by A. Alexeiff. Koschei can only be killed if an egg containing the secret of his power is broken.

and it wove a spell of protection over Ivan, so that the water could not harm him. In fact, when Ivan was thrown into the boiling water, he came out stronger and more handsome than ever.

When the czar saw what a power of good the water had done Ivan, he thought, if I get into the cauldron, I will become young and strong again. So he jumped into the water and boiled to death.

Ivan was crowned czar in his place, married Princess Vasilisa, and they lived happily ever after.

The Black Bull of Norroway

I N NORROWAY, long ago, there lived a lady who had three daughters. One day the oldest daughter said to her mother, "Mother, bake me a bannock and roast me a collop, for I'm going away to seek my fortune."

Her mother did so, and the girl went away to an old witch washerwife and told her that she had come to seek her fortune. The witch told her that if she kept watch out the back door, her fortune would come. On the third day came a handsome man in a coach and six. "This one's for you!" said the witch.

So the girl got into the coach, which sped away.

The witch

The bull's brother's castle

The bull and the girl

A coach and six comes for the oldest girl

A coach and four comes for the second girl. But for the youngest comes a fearsome black bull that carries her off

HOME COOKING
The daughters ask for food traditionally eaten by Scottish travelers. A collop is a slice of meat and a bannock is an unsweetened cake made of oats. Bannocks were cooked on an iron hot-plate called a griddle, shown above.

The next day the second daughter arrived at the witch's house. When she looked out of the witch's back door, she saw a handsome man in a coach and four. "This one's for you!" said the witch.

Then the third daughter said to her mother, "Mother, bake me a bannock and roast me a collop, for I'm going away to seek my fortune." She went to the old witch washerwife and, like her sisters before her, kept watch from the back door for her fortune to come to her. Nothing came on the first day and nothing on the second. On the third, she saw a great black bull come bellowing down the road.

"This one's for you!" said the witch. The girl screamed in grief and fright. But the witch set her on the bull's back and away they went.

On and on they went until the girl was faint with hunger. The black bull said, "Eat out of my right ear and drink out of my left ear." She did as he said, and was wonderfully refreshed.

Then the bull went on again until they came to a splendid castle. "This castle belongs to my brother," said the bull. "We can rest here tonight." When they came to the castle, the bull's brother and his wife took the girl in and turned the bull out to graze in the park.

THE MIGHTY BULL
For farming peoples all over the world, the bull was (or is still) the major symbol of strength and fertility. This belief in the power of the bull was strong among the Celtic peoples of Europe. The black bull of this tale has many godlike qualities, including magically providing the girl with food and drink and fighting the devil.

In the morning they fetched the girl into a shining parlor, and gave her a fine apple, warning her not to bite into it until she was in the greatest trouble anyone had ever known.

After another long day's ride they came to a second castle. "This castle belongs to my second brother," said the bull. "We can rest here tonight." In the morning, the people of the castle gave the girl a fine pear, warning her not to bite into it until she was in the greatest trouble anyone had ever known.

At the end of the third day they came to another castle, the biggest one yet. "My youngest brother lives here," said the bull. At that castle, they gave the girl a fine plum, warning her not to bite into it until she was in the greatest trouble anyone had ever known.

The bull's brother and his wife give the girl a magic apple

The next morning the bull and the girl rode on until they came to a dark glen. The bull set the girl down and said, "Now I must go and fight the devil. Sit on that stone and do not move hand or foot until I return. If you move, I will never be able to find you again. If all about you turns blue, you will know I have beaten the devil. But if all about you turns red, the devil will have beaten me."

THE HIGH ROAD
The heroine of this Lowland tale seems to be journeying north, past castles like Dundarave on Loch Fyne, toward the snow-capped mountains of the Highlands.

By the blue light, she realizes the bull has defeated the devil. She makes a fatal movement.

BEATING THE DEVIL
The devil, here pictured by Frank C. Papé in *The Book of Psalms* (1914), may be beaten in this story, but he is never far away in British folklore. A dropped fork, spilled water, or salt all attract him, although you may drive him away if you throw a pinch of spilled salt over your left shoulder and thus into his eyes. Yawning can be dangerous, for if you do not place your hand over your mouth, the devil may fly in.

The girl sat on the stone and didn't move a muscle. After a long time, everything around her turned blue and, in her joy at the bull's victory, she crossed one leg over the other.

Now the bull was really the Duke of Norroway, who had been enchanted into the shape of a black bull until he defeated the devil. Because the girl had moved, he could not find her when he came back from the fight.

The girl sat for a long time, weeping all alone. At last she got up and set off, she didn't know where to.

On she wandered until she came to a great hill of glass. She tried to climb it, but she couldn't. She tried to walk around it, but she couldn't. At last she came to a smithy, and the smith promised her that if she would serve him for seven years, he would make her a pair of iron shoes with which she could climb the glass hill. And at the end of seven years he was as good as his word, and the girl climbed the glass hill in her iron shoes.

When she reached the top, she found herself back in the witch washerwife's hut! "Wash these shirts," the witch said, "and I'll help you find your true love." The witch did not tell her that the shirts, which were stained with the devil's blood, belonged to the Duke of Norroway, who had sworn to marry the girl who could wash them clean. The witch had tried, her daughter had tried, but neither could shift the stains. But when the girl tried, the shirts were spotlessly clean.

The witch took the shirts to the duke, and told him that her daughter had washed them clean. So the Duke of Norroway and the witch's daughter were to be married.

When the girl realized she had been tricked, she thought of the beautiful apple she had been given and, biting into it, discovered it was filled with gold and silver jewelry. She went to the witch's daughter and said, "If you will delay your wedding one day, and allow me to go to the duke's room tonight, you can have these jewels."

The witch's daughter agreed, but the witch prepared a sleeping drink for the duke, so the girl could not awaken him.

The girl climbs the hill of glass

The shirts come out spotless

The next day the girl opened the pear, and found it full of jewels even more magnificent than those in the apple. She made her bargain again with the witch's daughter, but once more the witch gave the duke a sleeping draft, and she could not awaken him.

On the third day, the duke went hunting. His friends asked him about the crying and sighing coming from his bedroom the past two nights. The puzzled duke replied that he hadn't heard a thing.

Meanwhile, the girl opened the plum, and found jewelry even richer than that in the pear. She bargained as before, and the witch prepared another sleeping drink for the duke; but this time the duke, suspecting a trick, threw the drink away without tasting it.

CUNNING WITCH
The witch washerwife, also known as the "henwife," is the traditional witch of Scottish storytelling. She is more of a wise woman, cunning in the arts of medicine and magic, than an out and out villainess.

The duke is made to think that the witch's daughter cleaned the shirts

The sleeping duke

The jewels persuade the witch's daughter to let the girl spend time with the duke

The duke had just dozed off to sleep when the girl came into his room, sat by his side, and sang:

"Seven long years I served for thee,
The glassy hill I climbed for thee,
The bloody shirt I wrang for thee,
Will you not waken and turn to me?"

The duke awoke and turned to her. She told him all that had befallen her since they had parted, and he told her all that had befallen him. And he cast off the witch and her daughter and married the girl, and maybe they are still happily together today.

On the third night, the duke hearkens to the girl's sad song

Index

Acknowledgments

Key: l=left, r=right, t=top, c=center, a=above, b=below

The publisher would like to thank the following for their kind permission to reproduce the photographs:

AKG Photo: 150tl; British Museum, London 132b ; Dresden Gemäldegalerie, Alte Meister: *Im Wirtshaus*, David Teniers (1610–1690) 79; from *The Fisherman and His Wife*, P. Hey (1867–1952) 81tr ; *Suleiman the Magnificent*, 1530–40 Titian School, © Erich Lessing 96tl; *Peter I, the Great*, I. M. Nikitin (1690–1741) 152tl; *Trat ein Bursche in den Reigen*, 1902, A.P. Rabuschkin 104clb; *The Witch*, 1870, Hans Thoma 12br; *The Village of Thy Nguyen, 1958* 70; *Wilhelm IV of Bavaria, Tournament Vienna 1515* 94
American Museum of Natural History: 106bl; 145
© Bildarchiv Preussischer Kulturbesitz, Berlin: 15tl
Bildhuset, Ake Eison Lindman: 62
BFI Stills, Posters and Designs: United Artists (1942) 91
The Bridgeman Art Library, London: Chris Beetles Ltd., London: *Trinidad*, by Albert Goodwin (1845–1932) 55 ; Bible Society, London: *Seven-headed Serpent* , from the Book of Revelations, Luther Bible (c.1530) 95; Bonhams, London: *Indian seven-jeweled necklace* 140; British Library, London: *Arabian Nights*, "He Saw a Genie of Monstrous Bulk," by René Bull (d. 1942) 13tr, 102; British Library, London: *Border Detail of a Mermaid and a Tinker* 138bl; Christie's Images: *The Alchemist at Work*, by David Teniers the Elder (1582–1649) 52b; The Maas Gallery, London: *The Stuff That Dreams Are Made Of*, by John Anster Fitzgerald (1832–1906) 10; Manchester City Art Galleries: *Cupid & Psyche* by Sir Edward Burne-Jones 41tr; Private collection: *Duleep Singh, Maharajah of Lahore*, 1854 by Franz Xavier Winterhalter (1806–73) 141; private collection: *Genesis 28: 10 Jacob's Ladder*, Nuremberg Bible (1483) 109
By Permission of the British Library, London: *Shelfmark G17758* 88tl; *Shelfmark C57.a.20* 114
The British Museum, London: 66
© Neil Campbell-Sharpe: 38tl
Jean Loup Charmet: 14tc ; 104tl
Bruce Coleman Ltd.: Alain Compost 93; M. Diggin 83; Christer Fredriksson 120; Stephen J. Krasemann 144clb; Gordon Langsbury 78cl; Claudio Marigo 47br; William S. Paton 155tr; Mary Plage 42; Staffan Widstrand 34
Sue Cunningham Photographics: 48tl ; 48bl
Michael Diggin Photography: 83
Ecoscene: James Marchington 138tl
E.T. Archive: 69 ; 72tl
Mary Evans Picture Library: 11br; 13tl; 15cla; 18tl; 23; 32tl; 56bl; 61br; 74bl; 99; 121; 122tl; 122bl; 125; 128; 156cl; 161br
Chris Fairclough Colour Library : 76bl
Ffotograff: © Patricia Aithie 75
The Finnish Tourist Board: 136
Werner Forman Archive: Metropolitan Museum of Art, New York 74tl ; Museum für Volkenkunde 118tl
Fortean Picture Library/Janet & Colin Bord: 24
Garden Picture Library: Brian Carter 54
Ronald Grant Archive: 40tl; 117; 130bl; © Disney Enterprises, Inc. 15crb; © Disney Enterprises, Inc. 124

Guildhall Art Gallery, Corporation of London: 157
Robert Harding Picture Library: 18bl, 45tr, 49, 135; Kathy Collins 78bl; © Carol Jopp 147tr; Mike Newton 92; Ellen Rooney 155br; Bildagentur Schuster, Schmied 106tl
Michael Holford: 76tl; 143tr
Hulton Getty: 84clb
Hutchison Library: © A. Eames 100
Images Colour Library/Charles Walker Collection: 12bl
Palace/NFFC/ITC (courtesy Kobal) 89
Magnum: H. Gruyaert 137
Manchester City Art Galleries: *A Winter Night'sTale*, D. Maclise 14bl
© Musées Royaux des Beaux Art de Belgique, Bruxelles/ © Koninklijke Musea voor Schone Kunsten van Belgie, Brussel: *Anthropomorphic Landscape, Portrait of a Man*, Dutch School 16th century 11ca
Museum of London: 116
Reproduced by courtesy of the Trustees of the National Gallery, London: *A Grotesque Old Woman*, Quinten Massys (1465–1530) 96bl ; *The Vision of the Blessed Gabriel*, detail, Carlo Crivelli (c. 1430/1435–94) 27
Det Nationalhistoriske Museum på Frederiksborg, Hillerod: *Portrait of Hans Christian Andersen*, 1834 Albert Küchler 15tr
National Maritime Museum: 61tr
Natural History Photographic Agency : E. A. Jones 82
Peter Newark's American Pictures: 65
Peter Newark's Western Americana: 144tl; 146
Opie Collection. Bodleian Library, Oxford: 107tr
Oxford Scientific Films: © Paul Franklin 22; © David Curl 112bl; © Jorge Sierra Antinolo 150cl
Panos Pictures: J. C. Callow 118bl
Photostage: © Donald Cooper: 43
Real Academia de San Fernando, Madrid: 111br
Rex Features: Michael Friedel 72bl; © Ross Bray, Wildtrek Media 112tl
Royal Albert Memorial Museum: 119
Scala: 12tr
Science & Society Picture Library: 91tr
The Slide File: 29 ; 30 ; 31
Sotheby's Picture Library: 38cl
South American Pictures/Tony Morrison: 47tr
Leslie E. Spatt: 20
Tony Stone Images: 59; Darryl Torckler 101; Hans Peter Huber 81crb; Paul Harris 142; Robert Frerck 143br
Tate Gallery, London: *Oberon, Titania, and Puck*, c.1785 William Blake (1757–1827) 13br
Topham Picture Source: 113
Tokyo National Museum: 45br
Trip: Ibrahim 57; W. Jacobs 68; N. Price 151; H. Rogers 56tl
Reproduced by courtesy of the Trustees of the Victoria and Albert Museum: 147crb
Rex Whistler: *Reversable Head of Cinderella and the Godmother*, c. 1935, Estate of Rex Whistler 1996, all rights reserved, DACS 130tl
Rodney Wilson: 16-17c; 50-51c; 85 ; 86-87c; 126-127c
Zefa: 98, 134

DK would like to thank:

Lynn Bresler for the index, and Janet Allis for design assistance.